Therapy for the Dead

by Penny Johnston

Penny Johnston, Publisher

© Copyright 2015 by Penny Johnston

All rights reserved. No part of this publication may be reproduced, stored in a retrieval system, distributed or transmitted, in any form or by any means, electronic, mechanical, photocopying, recording, or otherwise without the prior written permission of the copyright owners. The scanning, uploading and distribution of this book via the Internet, or via any other means, without the permission of the publisher, is illegal and punishable by law. Please purchase only authorized electronic editions, and do not participate in or encourage electronic piracy of copyrighted materials. Your support of the authors' rights is appreciated.

Penny Johnston, Publisher

The characters and events in this book are fictitious. Any similarity to real persons, living or dead, is coincidental and not intended by the author.

ISBN 978-0-9939979-0-7

Also issued as ISBN 978-0-9939979-2-1 (epub)
and 978-0-9939979-1-4 (mobi)

Cover Design by Sara Carrick

Detective and Mystery stories, Canadian (English). Johnston, Penny

Dedicated to The late Lillian Boyd Uren Johnston Madill, Richard and Wendy Johnston

Acknowledgements

Thank you to Robert Barnett (cover photo), Lilie Funk, editor and cover artist Sara Carrick

Penny Johnston

Try as she might, she couldn't get back to sleep. She tossed and turned, pulling the flannel sheets and blanket up to cover her face, and then pulling them down again. She was hot, next thing she was too cold. Then through the eerie darkness in her room, she heard a noise. She lay perfectly still and listened. Where did it come from? There it was again. It was the sound of metal scraping on the front door lock, followed by the rattle of the door handle. Someone was breaking in. Almost paralyzed with fear, she wondered what would happen next? After a while the noise stopped. What was there to steal? The only valuable thing she had was her Panasonic TV in the living room which she had bought ten years ago. There it was again. The old lady lay on her bed waiting and wondering what to do next.

    This had been going on for several nights.

    She got up slowly tiptoeing over to the living room's front window and pulled back the cotton drape ever so slightly peering out, so that she could see who it was without being noticed. She looked over to her right to her front door. It was hard to see but the overhead porch light helped her to make out a tall male figure at her door dressed in black jeans, and black head covered hoodie which prevented her from seeing his face.

    "I'm going to call the police," she shouted. With that the figure ran down her front walk and jumped into a car at the curb.

    She dialed 911. After twenty minutes, the police came in a squad car, a long lapse of time which was most annoying. How were they going to catch anybody? The thief had long gone. They knocked on her front door. The two of them after flashing their badges and giving their names as Greg something or other and Clancy sauntered in, and very nonchalantly sat down on the sofa in the living room and with a bored look on their faces that clearly said why bother us. The one called Greg took out his pen and notebook and wrote in the date, the time of day, then waited for her to say something. The other one sat with his hands folded. She explained it all like she had on the phone. Then they went outside and looked at the lock on the front door. They tried the handle several times. Greg then closed his notebook. "Nothing to worry about, Miss Temple. Phone us, the next time, you hear him at your door. Probably some kid that lives in the neighbourhood. He didn't get in, did he? That's the main thing. Your sharp ears kept the wolf from the door." They smiled at their little joke and then they got up to go. "Phone us the next time you hear anything and we'll be right over."

How patronizing they are! I could have been murdered in my bed and what would they care thought Miss Temple when they had gone. I am old anyway ready for the Grand Reaper. In their minds, I am ready to be placed on the slag heap ready to push up daisies.

She went into her small kitchen, and put on the kettle for a cup of tea to soothe her shattered nerves. After drinking it slowly, she went back to bed and tried to sleep.

But sleep did not come easily. Someone out there was trying to break in and might kill her.

*****

Over at the Sandy household, Mrs. Sandy was sipping her Earle Grey Breakfast tea pondering the meaning of life. Opposite her at the breakfast table, Dr. Sandy was chewing his buttered toast.

"I think Miss Temple has gone missing. It's not like her to leave her newspapers on the doorstep, or her mail uncollected in the mail box. I went around to her house when she didn't show up at the church. She was supposed to lead us in Bible Study. She had phoned about it just the other day wanting my suggestions on some biblical passages. She's very reliable and conscientious about everything. It's not like her to suddenly not show up. I'm going to phone one of her neighbours, Mrs. Brown and see if they have seen her. It may be cause for alarm."

Mrs. Brown was not much more enlightening. "Well I talked to her yesterday and she said she was going for a walk on the Trans Canada Trail in north Mariposa. I haven't heard from her since. I knocked on her door but she didn't answer. I used the key under the mat to go in and check but she was nowhere to be found. I see one of two flyers piling up on her doorstep along with her newspaper. Haven't you heard anything?"

"Me neither."

"Suppose she tripped on a tree root, fell and broke her ankle or her hip on the trail or had a heart attack? She is elderly and anything can happen. She might have had a stroke. Anything is possible. She might have gotten lost or very confused after she had fallen."

"I think we should organize a search party to find her, beginning with the Trans Canada Trail where she last went walking. The first thing that we must do, though, is to notify the police."

She phoned the Mariposa OPP and spoke to Clancy Murphy who although he didn't sound enthusiastic, didn't pooh, pooh, her fears. "She is a tiny woman, with a mind that is crystal clear. She is not demented like so many her age who wander off and get lost. She may have placed herself in harm's way."

"Right," said Clancy "The weather looks good for this afternoon, and a couple of the lads have some spare time. We can put a search party together. How about it? Tell everyone to assemble at the beginning of the trail by the waterfront. I will notify the radio station about what we are going to do."

* * * * *

The Trans Canada Trail was a forest of towering white pine, leafy maple, and shady oak trees, frequented by raccoons, white tailed deer, and owls. Mushrooms, sodden grass, leaves, bits of pine needles, twigs, and sand hugged the forest's floor.

A large group of, neighbours, friends of Miss Temple, and women from the church, gathered in front of Clancy who was standing in front of a large white marquee tent which had been set up on the waterfront. He addressed the crowd. "In this tent, we have set up a command post. We will have food and water available for those who need it.

"First of all, I want you to sign in on this clipboard, and at the end of the search to sign out, so that nobody gets lost. What we are looking for, is a small old lady with white hair, height about 1.5 metres weighing about 45 kg. She was last seen yesterday telling her friends that she was going to go for a walk along the Trans Canada Trail that snakes along the shoreline of Lake Couchiching. She may have wandered off the trail, looking at a special wild flower, or a migratory bird, so we want you to separate, and fan out. We have made a grid of the property that we are going to look at."

On the grid he showed them how he wanted them to proceed in small groups, separated by several metres.

"Take along a walking stick to poke holes in the piles of brush, debris, anything and everything is important. Look for a missing shoe, a scarf, a purse etc.

Poke holes underneath creek beds etc.

We'll set the dog out and see if he can pick up a scent. She may have gotten disorientated, and lost."

"Not Miss Temple." A woman from the crowd corrected him. "She's as sharp as a knife in a drawer. There are no flies on her. All her knives are sharp in the drawer."

David Scott drifted over to the table. "Do you need any help?"

"Got your water bottle?" asked Clancy, "I want you to go out with the gang. Give me a report as you go along to tell me how you are doing."

Fifteen minutes later, Clancy gave David a ring on his cell phone, "Find anything?"

"Lots of dog turds and raccoon droppings. I saw a large osprey nest in a tree. A deer with her young ran across the trail ahead of us." Then he paused and looked around. "There are quite a few birds; woodpeckers, robins, sparrows, flying overhead. As we were speaking a woodchuck just wandered across the trail."

"I am not interested in your feathered friends. This ain't the Audubon Society. Keep looking. Keep turning over the stuff on the ground."

"Will do. It is very boring, frustrating work, turning over piles of leaves and turds looking for a body. You hope you will find something. So far nobody has found anything. We'll search for an hour and see what turns up."

Clancy went over to the coffee table and helped himself to a whole wheat egg salad sandwich, something to munch on to kill the boredom.

Finished with the sandwich, and leaving the crusts for the birds to eat, he contacted David again. "Any word?"

"Nothing."

Then the dog began barking, pawing at his leash. His handler, another OPP officer, let it sniff Miss Temple's sweater again. The dog was good at it. The OPP office was full of trophies for canine finds.

Then Clancy heard his cell phone ring.

"David here."

"What have you got?"

"I think it is something but not what we were originally looking for. The tip of a large running shoe sticking out of a pile of debris by a fallen log covered by leaves. It looks like a man's running shoe by the size of it."

"What else do you see?"

"I see sneakers...big hairy legs. It's the body of a middle aged man who has been out jogging. We're just brushing off the leaves now."

"Stop right there. Tell me exactly where you are located. I'll be there in a jiffy. Don't touch anything. In the meantime, keep the crowd back. Don't disturb anything. We want to collect as much evidence as possible without disturbing what is there. Later we'll' have forensics sweep through the area. I'll call the coroner."

He thought to himself, it's funny but I don't recall hearing about a missing middle aged male.

Clancy walked up to the spot on the trail and joined his men where the body lay on the ground. When he got there, he got another officer to block off the area with yellow duct tape on the trees. "Call off the search. Get the volunteers out of here."

He didn't want a crowd of gawkers looking over his shoulder messing up the crime scene and leaving their DNA around for them to collect.

"How long do you think he has lain there?"

"Until the coroner comes we won't know for sure. The development of insects on his body will tell us how long he has been there. It doesn't look like too long. The body is well preserved considering this is a hot day. There is no damage to his face."

Another constable came up and glanced down at the body. "I recognize him; it looks a lot like Jerry Lang, a local psychiatrist. I could be mistaken, though."

"Someone should have missed him. Any ID on him?"

"None. No pockets in his T-shirt and he is not wearing a jacket. Will take a photo."

"How was he killed?"

"When we rolled him over, I noticed a bloody tear in his shirt and dried blood which had seeped into his clothes. It looks like a slit was done by a knife. He was stabbed to death."

"Mm," thought Clancy, "If someone got stabbed in the back from behind, he would have had to stop to talk to someone and then in turning got stabbed or it could be another jogger coming up from behind, catching up with him. But then he would have heard him coming. Do you see any blood on the ground?"

"There is a lot of detritus, leaves, twigs, mushrooms, and mold covering the ground which makes it difficult to spot because the blood would now be brown spots. It rained last night for about a half an hour so any blood would be washed away. Off hand, I don't see any. If we can't find any blood here, it means he may have been killed elsewhere and dumped here. But it would be difficult to drag him in here, a heavy body like this, and hide his body without some other jogger or someone walking on the trail seeing this being done. The trail is very public. Someone must have seen something. If there is lividity in his lower limbs or torso it means he was killed and then moved here. The coroner will tell us.

"How did he get here? Did he jog here? Or did he come by car? Check the concession road that intersects the trail just a few metres away for a parked car. Check for blood stains on the gravel around the car."

A few minutes later, David called back. "Clancy, there is only one car parked here by the side of the road. It looks like it has been parked overnight with rain streaks on the windshield. There are no bloodstains to be found on the gravel."

"Put a coat hanger in the window and get this car unlocked. If it is his car, his ID is probably left behind when he went jogging. His ID and his cell phone are probably stashed in the glove compartment. I'll call the coroner."

Back at the tent, Clancy spoke to the assembled crowd. "Listen up, everybody. I want to make an announcement. Thanks for all your trouble. You can all go home now. We've found a body which we didn't expect to find. We don't know who it is except that it is a middle aged male. That's all I can tell you at this point until the next of kin identifies the body. Miss Temple has still not been found.

"Excuse me, my phone is ringing."

"This is Soldiers Memorial Hospital here in Mariposa. An old lady was brought in, unconscious with a big bump on the back of her head. She was found at the side of the road. It might be the old lady you are looking for. Send someone over to identify her."

"Thanks. Will do. David you are good with the old ladies. You have a nice bedside manner. I am sending you over to Soldiers Memorial. Take Mrs. Sandy with you to identify an old lady whom we think is Miss Temple. She is in emergency.

"As for this new case on our hands, it will mean interviewing professionals, doctors and the like. It will require diplomacy and tact which I believe I possess. I have the necessary skills set for this kind of investigation.

"First I'll have to notify the next of kin. It's funny that the wife, if he is married didn't notify us that he was missing? The immediate suspects would be someone close to him, like his family. We also have to look at his colleagues, the people he worked with and last but not least his patients. I'll be doing a lot of work and will need your help. Bob White over in Barrie is useless, all talk and no action."

David rolled his eyes heavenward. Tact and diplomacy, that's a laugh, Fat Clancy was an elephant in a china shop when interviewing people.

Clancy grinned, "David, you have a nice manner with little old ladies, how about you find out more about what happened to Miss Temple."

"I'll consider that statement a compliment."

David drove straight over to emergency and parked in the ambulance parking spot in the breezeway. At the desk sat a cute young nurse with dimples in her cheeks and a wide pepsodent smile. "I have come to see about that old lady, the one we were searching for. I got a call from the hospital telling me that it might be her."

"Bingo! It's your lucky day." She smiled. "We think we have her here, She was brought in yesterday late in the day suffering from amnesia. She has a bad concussion on the back of her head. She didn't know who she was, where she lived or anything at all. She was found by the concession road intersecting with the Trans Canada Trail. I don't know how long she lay there, a few hours or a day at the most. I think she must be the old lady you're looking for. She's a real odd bird."

"Did she give her age?"

"No, she has no ID, nothing on her not even a handbag."

"I'll get somebody over who knows her. Mrs. Sandy, her neighbour, can identify her. On his cell phone he contacted Mrs. Sandy. "I think we have found her. Can you come and identify her?"

"Is she alright?"

"No memory of anything that has happened to her and her handbag is gone. At least she is alive."

"Yes, I will be glad to come. I'll drive over to the hospital and meet you there in about 15 minutes."

At reception the attending nurse took them along the corridor, dodging a mix of trolleys carrying food trays, medicines and bedpans. David tried not to breathe in the smell. They took the crowded elevator, with patients and visitors up to the third floor to the old lady's room which she shared with another patient. The nurse drew the white curtains aside and pulled back the covers on her bed. "We are monitoring her vital signs for the next twenty found hours, in case of a hematoma on the brain. She awoke just briefly this morning." He could see that she was hooked up to the electrocardiograph machine which was beeping away with its regular hill and valleys. An IV with saline solution and an antibiotic drip was attached to her scrawny thin arm.

The old lady was lying sleeping curled up in a fetal position, her white hair held in place by a large bandage. He noticed the scrapes and insect bite marks on her arms. She also had several nasty bruises on her face and neck.

Mrs. Sandy peered down at her face for a minute. "That's her. Yes, I am quite sure that is Miss Temple. She needs her rest after what she has been through. She is lucky to be alive. How did they find her?"

"A truck driver got out of his cab to relieve himself in a shallow ditch by the side of the road. There he found her at his feet, dirty and dusty, and unconscious. At first he thought she was dead, so he called 911. The ambulance came and brought her here.

She was unconscious from the blow to the back of her head. She had been there all night. But it was a warm night and she didn't suffer from exposure. We are monitoring her vital signs and looking for any internal bleeding. She came to this morning and we questioned her briefly, but she is tired from all that outdoor exposure. She can't remember a thing."

"Why would she be found near a concession road?"

"She was probably hit over the head, and then tossed into the ditch with the driver speeding off. He probably left her for dead."

"What a dreadful way to treat an old lady. Harmless, too," murmured Mrs. Sandy.

"If she was so harmless, why was she attacked? She probably had very little money in her purse. Old ladies are not known for carrying around stashes of cash. Something tells me it wasn't robbery. It was something else," said David.

"Nurse, when she comes to and able to talk, I would like

to come back and have a few words with her. Here is my card."

"She might not be too helpful. The trauma of her injuries would make her forget everything."

"At least I can try."

"Do you think Mrs. Sandy, that this could have happened somewhere along the Trans Canada Trail?"

"It could be. It was near the place, she said she was going for a walk."

"It's a coincidence that we discovered a body on the trail and this was the last place, we assume that Miss Temple was walking."

"I agree with you. But we will have to wait until she is conscious."

"Thanks for your help, Mrs. Sandy. We'll have to wait and see." David headed back to the office.

* * * * *

Back at the office, Clancy sat down in his swivel chair and rotated it a couple of times while deep in thought. Try as he might his recurring thoughts were not on solving the murder but on his dog. "I took my dog in for a checkup over to the vet. I told you he has not been eating and acting poorly. The vet wants $1,500 to operate, cash in advance or installments of $500.00 per deposit. This is highway robbery. Bank robbers don't even get these amounts from the teller. Vets make more money than doctors and they keep it hush, hush, hush. The swine! Human beings are not as important as animals in this world. I have a big murder case to solve and how can I concentrate with this hanging over my head?"

"Things are tough all over. Get used to it. What have we established so far in this investigation?" asked David.

"Boy, you're dripping with sympathy. Remind me the next time your hand gets caught in a car door. To put you in the picture, David, Jerry Lang the psychiatrist got stabbed. Someone approached him and stabbed him either after talking to him or came up from behind. I think he was killed close to where we found him. We'll know for sure from the coroner if the body had been moved after death. I can't see the perp getting away unnoticed by creeping up behind him on the concession road where Dr. Lang's car was parked. There is no cover to hide behind on that road, just weeds and a deep ditch running on both sides. The forest of trees is further back by several metres. It would not be possible to hide there and wait. So his attacker couldn't hide in the brush. So either he came along the trail from an unknown direction and my guess would be that there was some confrontation or such, that he knew his attacker, someone who could get that close to him. But I am just guessing. We'll put up a poster, plastering them all over town, asking for anyone who saw anything on Friday 13th between 3.30 and 5.30 p.m.

"Now there doesn't seem to be any signs of a struggle, no defense wounds or bruises or knife wounds on his forearms or arms. We'll have to wait for the coroner to find out if there was blood or skin under his fingernails which would be there if he was fighting off somebody. He must have known his attacker and this stabbing took him by surprise."

"Why was he stabbed in the back? Why not in the front? Why not in the chest?"

"Don't know. Luckily we were searching for Miss Temple and accidentally found the body, otherwise the body would not have been discovered for several days.

"If it had lain there longer, the wild animals would have torn the body apart. It was a lucky break for us. Eventually he would have been found because his car was parked near there and someone would have noticed the dust on the car and that the car had been parked there awhile. Then an immediate search of the area would have found him.

Was this a random attack by a deranged patient who knew that Lang would be jogging at that time of day and that he was a regular on the trail? So any patient that he saw in the hospital or in his office could have killed him. It could have been his wife, his secretary, any colleagues. We have a lot of work ahead of us including advising his widow."

* * * * *

"Hot isn't it? I think we are getting a heat wave. It's

early for June. Can we turn on the air conditioner?" David had rolled up his shirt sleeves and loosened his tie so he could be more comfortable sitting at his desk.

"You're acting like a little old lady who has hot flashes. Hydro is expensive. We have to save on hydro."

"I'm not. I am just being reasonable," said David. Really sometimes Clancy was too much.

"Well I have to go and tell the widow the good news before the press gets hold of it. It's not a pleasant scene and then have her identify the body," He picked up his cell phone. "Clancy Murphy of Mariposa OPP. I have something important to tell you, Mrs. Lang. Will you be in so I can come over right now? The matter is urgent."

"Of course, but what is it about? Is it anything serious?"

"I prefer to inform you in person."

Clancy drove up the circular driveway to a large Victorian house with stained glassed windows in the stairwell, fronting a large expanse of lawn. Someone would have to be hired to cut that much grass, Dr. Lang, wouldn't have time to do that. He got out, stretched his legs, and then headed up the flagstone path to the front door. He pressed the bell setting off a series of chimes.

First he heard the yip, yap of a small dog running towards the door its toenails scratching the hardwood floor. He wasn't kept waiting long. Behind the dog, came Mrs. Lang, who opened the door, dressed in Bermuda shorts and a pink T-shirt. She was a pretty blue eyed a blond, about 1.70 metres tall and stacked in all the right places. She bent down to pick up a white haired blow dried Pekinese dog with two tiny pink bows in its hair obscuring its eyes. How he hated pretentious little dogs and women who fussed over them.

He showed her his ID. "I have some bad news to deliver to you. Can we find a place to sit down?"

"In here." She waved her hand in the direction of the living room. It was a large room with a few oil paintings. A DeBoers white leather sofa and chairs were arranged comfortably around a fire place. A glass cabinet for drinks stood in a corner next to a floor to ceiling bookcase. He looked down at the white shag rug. Having a white rug and a dog was a luxury, and he had a dog which would ruin this rug in minutes.

He headed over to a spindly chair, with four legs, that screamed antique

"Don't," she said, "please not that one," she shouted. "It's fragile. It is an heirloom from my grandmother. It is so easy to break."

Embarrassed he moved towards the sofa and sank down amongst its cushions his body making squishing sounds as he sank.

"What is the news you have to tell me? I can't imagine anything that would be this important, for you to make a personal visit."

"It's your husband." He paused… "He's dead."

"You must have the wrong person. He is at a two medical day conference at the Marriott Hotel on Lake Rousseau. You can page him there."

A real swanky place for a conference, thought Clancy, Only the moneyed crowd have cottages there. They fly in by plane from Billy Bishop airport.

She picked up her cell phone. "I will contact the receptionist and have him paged." She waited letting the phone ring. "I have been paging him this morning but so far, I haven't got an answer. Maybe now he is free."

"We need you to identify the body, Mrs. Lang. We are pretty sure it's him. When did you last see your husband?"

"Yesterday at lunch. He saw patients in the morning and then for a couple of hours in the afternoon. Then he went jogging after which he was leaving for his medical conference."

"Did he come home between the time he went jogging and when he left for the Marriott?"

"He may have. I can't be sure. He never misses jogging. He loves the trail. He loves running. He prides himself on his physical fitness. How did you find the body? And why do you think it is my husband?"

"Mrs. Lang, we found a jogger's body hidden by leaves in the woods off the Trans Canada Trail this afternoon. We had a search party out for an elderly lady who had gone missing. We didn't find her but we believe we have found the body of your husband. His car was parked on Concession Road nearby."

"What kind of car?"

"A silver Lexus."

"Oh, oh, then there is a possibility it may be him." She paused and let the news sink in. She sat down and pulled out a handkerchief and dabbed at a tear that was slowly trickling down her cheek. "I can't believe it." She shook her head. "I'm in shock."

"Can I get you a glass of water?"

"Water? No, I don't want water. I need a strong drink. Pour me a whisky in that shot glass over there." He walked over to the cabinet, poured her one and then handed it to her. She threw back her head and gulped it down. "That's better. So it could be my husband. How was he killed?"

"He was stabbed to death."

"Oh, how awful."

"Will you come with me?"

"Yes. Give me a few minutes to get my things." She locked the door, bringing with her a pink leather shoulder purse and her cell phone.

"Do you mind if I take your arm? I feel unsteady on my feet." She grabbed his elbow.

"Most certainly, Mrs. Lang. This will take just a few minutes of your time." He led her to the car, opened the door and she got in. He drove down to the hospital morgue which was in the basement. Then they walked along the grey tiled corridor to the viewing room. "Are you ready, Mrs. Lang?"

"I will never be ready for this."

They waited while the gurney was wheeled out. When they lifted the sheet from his face, Mrs. Lang lurched forward. "Yes, that's my husband," she sobbed. "Yes, that's Jerry." Then she closed her eyes and slumped to the floor.

Clancy fortunately caught her on the way down. When she opened her eyes this time he gave her a glass of water. "I have arranged for one of the women constables to take you back to your residence and make you a nice cup of tea." Mrs. Lang nodded

"Mrs. Lang we must talk later. It is quite a shock. I will

drop by when you are rested to see how you are doing and ask a few more questions."

Clancy returned to the office and informed the officers that the widow, Mrs. Lang had formally identified her husband, Dr. Jerry Lang. We should tell Mira of Mariposa Packet, and ask her for her help. You used to be in tight with her David, maybe you will get more mileage than I could out of her."

"I doubt it. Mira has given me the deep chill lately."

"Whatever did you do?" purred Clancy." Was it just slam, bam, thank you ma'am? I thought you were a gentleman. I'm all ears."

"I'll bet you are. Mira cooled things when I started dating Clara Clarke. You can't have two women at the same time. She told me "I'm a one woman man. Make a choice."

"I see," said Clancy, "then it is up to me to contact her. Mira can be very helpful or she can be a real bitch. She needs a real man like me to warm her heart."

David smiled to himself. "Go to it. What's she like, this Mrs. Lang?" asked David.

"Well she is high maintenance, a looker and a bit spoilt. She's not a meat and potatoes woman."

"What on earth is a meat and potatoes woman?" asked David his curiosity aroused.

"Well I have been married ten years and I would describe my wife as a meat and potatoes woman, plain but no frills. A substantial meal but no trimmings if you get my meaning. To give you an example, every time I had to drive to Toronto for a meeting there was this woman always standing half way down the street, just standing there on Jarvis facing the oncoming traffic. She wasn't hitching a ride. She was just standing there. She was plain, had very little make up on, in her early forties, I'd say. She was a meat and potatoes woman and obviously there was a demand for her services. She was like the post.

* * * * *

After a nice quiet evening, Clancy felt refreshed and

ready to go the next day. He assessed the situation. He had to be a realist. Mister high and mighty, Senior Detective Bob White from Barrie had shown no sign of coming over to help in interviewing suspects nor did he offer. He was only a phone call away. "What good was he anyway? He was useless all chat and no action. We can't count on him. We've got to do the bloody work ourselves." said Clancy to no one in particular. "I am going back to interview Mrs. Lang again."

He drove up the circular driveway of the Lang house and parked. He noticed that the living room drapes had been drawn. The house looked forlorn. The gas lamp by the front door was still on. A curtain was pulled back on the front window and a shadowy figure was looking down at him.

He rang the bell, a set of chimes, which set the dog to barking.

The cleaning lady, in running shoes, wearing a white apron, holding a duster, who identified herself as Mrs. Parker, answered the door. "Mrs. Lang is resting "

"I need to talk to her. Get her."

"I will see if she wants to speak to you. It has been a great shock to all of us."

"Hello, hello, who is there?" A soft voice called out from upstairs.

"It's Detective Clancy Murphy. We spoke yesterday."

Mrs. Lang, with shadows under her eyes, her hair braided in a single blonde braid down the centre of her back came slowly down the stairs. He noticed that her hands were shaking, the blue veins standing out in contrast to her red nails. Her dog was barking at her heels.

"I am trying to get used to Jerry being gone. Do you mind if I have a glass of sherry before we start?" She went over to the glass cabinet and took out a crystal tumbler. Then she took the top off the decanter and poured a generous glass full. "I'd offer you a drink, but I know you don't drink on the job. Please sit down." She gestured to the sofa with her hand. He noticed a blinding diamond rock on her wedding finger. That ring must have cost a fortune.

"I want to trace Dr. Lang's actions on that final day. When did he leave the house?"

"In the morning around 9 o'clock. He came home for lunch around one for about forty five minutes and then went back to the office to see his patients."

"Did he come home to pick up his sports equipment? Did you see him again at that time?"

"If he came home, I didn't see him. No I am pretty sure of that. Mrs. Parker might have but I didn't."

"May I have Mrs. Parker's phone number? I want to have a few words with her."

"I don't see what that bow legged bitch can tell you. She just does chores."

"Let me be the judge of that." He wrote down her telephone number and put it in his notebook for further reference. May I have a brief word with her?"

"I'll get her if you think that will be any help." Mrs. Lang flounced off

Mrs. Parker came slowly down the hall to meet him, a wet mop in her hands with a faint smell of javex clinging to her clothing. Beyond her, he could see Mrs. Lang lingering in the background trying to overhear their conversation.

"Mrs. Parker how about we meet at Tim Horton's after your shift today? I won't keep you long. There are some questions I want to ask you."

"Me? That's very flattering of you to want to ask my opinion," said Mrs. Parker, smoothing her hair and straightening her apron. "I'm only the cleaning lady here. I know next to nothing."

"In a murder investigation, everything helps." Clancy headed back to his office to see if any messages or any witnesses had come forward. So far Zip.

* * * * *

Promptly at 3.30, he parked his car in the Tim Horton's parking lot. Went in, looking around for Mrs. Parker. She was easily identifiable with her candy white spun hair and dressed in a plain blue pantsuit sitting in a booth. Mrs. Parker, he judged to be in her sixties, long ready for retirement but without the funds to enjoy it.

He slid into the seat opposite her. "Glad you could come. I hope you had no difficulty getting here. Can I get you a cup of tea?"

'Yes, thank you that would be nice. I don't know what I can tell you. I just clean the house for Mrs. Lang.

"How long have you been cleaning the house for her?"

"Ever since she moved into this house. About three years. There's a lot to clean."

"What is she like to work for?

"Well I do my work and I try to say as little as possible around her. She has a mean streak. Most of the time, she is a bit of a bitch. I hope this conversation is confidential, just between the two of us, or I could lose my job." She glanced at him for a nod of agreement.

"I liked him more than I did her. She could be real mean at times. Complaining when I was late, saying she was going to deduct my pay. If I broke anything, she would take it out of my wages. Stuff like that. Everything had to be just so around her."

"Tell me about the 19th, the day Dr. Lang was murdered. What did you do from noon onwards?"

"Well I got the lunch ready for Dr. and Mrs. Lang, something simple like soup and sandwiches, carrots and celery sticks and put it out for them on the dining room table, along with fresh fruit for dessert. Then I left the two of them to eat and chat. I went to vacuum the living room rug and then tidy up in the hall."

"What was Dr. Lang's demeanor like? Was he in a good mood or what? Was he anxious or worried about anything?"

"He acted the same, his usual self, and very polite. They didn't seem to have much to say at the table. I heard him call out that he would be back for a change of clothes and to pick up his luggage before he went for a jog and then he would continue on to his conference at the Marriott. He usually jogged around 4, two to three days a week when he held office hours in Mariposa."

"So he was known to jog regularly?"

"Yes."

"The same place?"

"The Trans Canada Trail."

"Did you see him before he went?"

"I had left by the time he had come back to change. My day is over at 3 o'clock."

"Did you see Mrs. Lang again that afternoon?"

"No, she must have lain down for a nap or gone shopping. I take the bus outside their door and go home."

"What was she like that day?'

"She seemed more high strung. I put it down to her bad nerves. She seemed nervy to me. Do you know why she would be more high strung?"

"Nothing that I can think of. She never shares her troubles with me."

"What medication does she take?"

"I don't know. I haven't been into her medical cabinet in the bathroom. I have seen pill bottles out on her dresser but I have never really looked at them. I think she takes sleeping pills. I heard her say one day she says she needs them."

"Can you think of anyone who might want to murder Dr. Lang? Like a neighbor or a relative or someone within his circle?"

"He was a nice man and kind to everyone as far as I can see. No I can't."

"Well, Mrs. Parker thanks for your insight and help. If you can think of anything else, here's my card."

* * * * *

The phone rang.

"A caller for you, David," said Greg. "She sounds all sweetness and honey. This might be your lucky day."

"Oh come off it, Greg, Have you got only one thing on your mind?"

"I was just being helpful."

"Hello. David Scott, OPP here."

"Nurse Shelly of Soldiers Memorial. We met when you came to see and identify Miss Temple. She's coming around. Now would be a good time to talk to her. But keep it short. She tires easily."

"Thanks. I'll be right over."

From the hospital reception desk he found out her room number and joined a crowded elevator which took an irritating length of time to get there, stopping at each floor to let visitors and staff out along the way. An old geezer was standing in his hospital gown and slippers, his rear end half exposed. He was trying to squeeze himself onto the elevator. David looked up at the ceiling.

Nurse Shelly, a blue eyed, freckled cutie, was standing at the nurses' reception area, her stethoscope around her neck waiting for him. "Nice to see you again," she smiled.

"My pleasure. And the patient?"

She took him along the hall into the room where Miss Temple was sitting up with a rather dazed expression on her face and an IV drip in her right arm. Her hair had been combed and held in place with a hairpin. She didn't look as disheveled as she had previously. A bouquet of freshly cut orange Tiger Lilies was placed in water in a vase on her side table along with a glass of water.

"Miss Temple?"

"Yes?"

At least she knows her own name, thought David.

"How did I get here?"

"You were found by the roadside unconscious."

"Was I?"

"Yes. Can you remember anything that day? Like where you were that afternoon?"

"I went for a walk and that's all I can remember. Sometime in the afternoon after I had my nap, I went down onto the Trans Canada Trail by the lake. I can't remember anything more than that."

"What time? Did you take your purse? What was in your purse?"

"My purse. My purse. Where is it? Where has it gone?" Her hands fluttered in the air with great agitation.

David shook his head. "It has disappeared."

"I didn't have much money in it, but it held my health card, my hospital card and a credit card."

"Well they don't know your pin so they won't be able to

use your credit card or bank cards unless you have a simple pin, like 1, 2, 3, 4. It won't take long to get new health cards. Your doctor will have the OHIP card and number for the hospital. Do you remember meeting anyone?"

"My memory is no good. I am sorry." Miss Temple lay back exhausted on the pillow her eyes closed.

"That is enough, I am sorry," Nurse Shelly interrupted, "Miss Temple needs her rest. That is all she can remember. I hope it can be some help."

"It is not much to go on, that's for sure. At least we have established a time for when it happened. Thanks for your help." David left the room and headed back to the office. The murder of Dr. Lang and the attack on Miss Temple may be connected because they happened so close to each other. Maybe not. Was it just a coincidence? Only time will tell.

* * * * *

"Got a call for you, Clancy. It sounds like Dr. Frost. He has that superior tone of voice."

"Oh, no. He probably wants to schedule the autopsy of Dr. Lang for today. I have just had a full breakfast of bacon, eggs, toast and coffee. I don't know how I am going to handle it." He picked up the phone.

"Frost, here, I'll be doing the Lang autopsy bright and early at 10 a.m. sharp. Be there."

"Thanks for giving me advance notice." said Clancy and rung off.

"You can handle it," chirped Greg from his corner in the room." You are used to it."

"One is never used to a dead body."

Promptly at ten, he drove over to the hospital morgue He pressed a button and the automatic doors opened. Frost dressed in green scrubs, clipboard in hand was waiting for him. "Over here." The corpse of Dr. Lang was lying stretched out on the steel gurney, surrounded by draining ditches on all sides. Clancy glanced down at the body.

"How old would he be?"

"Forty eight."

"Well preserved. He looks much younger."

"What a waste. Let's get started. I have already weighed the body. Not an ounce of fat on him."

He lifted up the arms to examine them. No cut marks, no bruises. Just a few insect bites from being outdoors. I don't see any defense wounds, any attempts to fight off his attacker." He lifted up the hands, looking at the fingernails. "I'll swab them for blood, and skin in case he scratched the attacker. But it does not look as if he was in any fight. It seemed to be an attack that caught him by surprise. There's no blood pooling in the lower part of the body, so the body wasn't moved after death."

"Did he know his attacker?"

"That's up to you to determine."

Frost made the Y incision and then taking the electric saw cut through the rib cage to get at the bloody organs underneath. He lifted out the liver. "No sign of Cirrhosis. Spleen okay. Stomach contents. He had his last meal at noon. "Here's the heart." He weighed it. No signs of fatty tissue. He rolled the heart from side to side. The heart's in good shape, with no early hardening of the arteries.

Now here's what caused his death. A lucky stab from the back that pierced through his pulmonary artery. He bled to death from internal bleeding."

"What was the weapon? Any idea what kind of weapon was used?"

"Nothing unusual. Your average kitchen knife will do the trick."

He rolled Dr. Lang over on his back. There's the entry wound. He took a metal tape and put it into the wound. About five inches deep."

"So he could have been taken by surprise or he could have known the person and then turned his back on him."

"Your guess is as good as mine. Does that tell you anything?"

"It helps. Every little bit helps."

"I'll have to have you over for some wine and cheese soon. I keep forgetting."

Clancy mumbled that would be nice and headed out.

How can one think of food and drink over a dead body?

* * * * *

Searching through Dr. Lang's personal effects, which included the ID found in Jerry Lang's wallet was a staff card with his photo for Barrie General Hospital. Clancy wondered what were his relationships with his co-workers? How did he get on with members of the staff? Did anyone hold a grudge against him? Would he find the murder suspect among the patients or the co-workers of Barrie General? That tall building with several wings near the harbor. These were questions Clancy wanted to find out.

He started by phone at the top. He tried three times to get the medical director of Barrie General Hospital, and only succeeded in getting his secretary. "Dr. Eves is very busy seeing patients and attending meetings. I'll have Dr. Eves call you back. What number can you be reached at?" She sighed and waited for him to give her the number.

"It's important that I speak to him. Murder inquiries can't wait."

"I'll do my best but he is a busy man. As you can imagine, at the hospital, the patients concerns come first."

He waited for his call to be returned, and kept himself busy at the desk. Frustrated by not hearing from Dr. Eves, he decided to drive over to Barrie, about thirty minutes away and see if he could get an interview in person which would tell him more than a phone call. At the hospital, he found a space in the parking lot, parked his car and entered through the main entrance. In the hospital directory posted at the front door, he found the executive offices were located on the 6th floor. He took the elevator up and knocked on the medical director's door. The female receptionist, dressed in a pretty red sundress had been making doodles on a legal pad. She looked up.

"I have been trying to get hold of Dr. Eves. He hasn't returned my calls. So I came in person thinking I would have better luck. I am investigating a murder."

As luck would have it, Dr. Eves, a big burly man in a white lab coat came hurtling around the corner heading for his office door with an aside to his secretary. "Cancel my next appointment; I have something urgent that needs to be taken care of."

Clancy stepped in front of him blocking his way.

"Who on earth are you?" he sputtered. "How dare…?"

"A few minutes of your time, please, I'm Detective Clancy Murphy from the Mariposa Detachment investigating the murder of Dr. Jerry Lang."

"Oh, yes, I have been meaning to get back to you, my apologies."

"Dr. Jerry Lang was on your staff?"

"Yes, for three years. I would have suggested that you speak to public relations personnel but they didn't know him," said Dr. Eves. "Come into my office but I won't ask you to sit down. I am in a big rush today."

"Jerry Lang, what can you tell me about him?"

"Basically I had no complaints about him. He was very capable. The patients liked him; he had a nice bedside manner, no problems all the time he was here. I could write a recommendation for him any day."

"He met his second wife here?"

"Yes, she worked in the addiction clinic."

"Do you have any idea what his first wife was like?"

"That was before he came here, He was here just a short when he got a divorce. Before he practiced in London, Ontario and at University College Hospital. I gather the divorce like most divorces was unpleasant."

"Would you care to comment further?"

"I don't know more. That's all I can tell you. "

"Have you any idea of anyone who might want to murder him?"

"None what so ever. Why not give Dr. Coldwater a ring. He has a private practice in Mariposa and was a lifelong friend of Jerry's. He might give you further insight."

"Thanks, will do."

Dr. Eves' secretary didn't even look up from her desk as Clancy made his way out

We could interview half of Mariposa and get no further ahead thought Clancy Obviously his patients in Barrie would not know that he went jogging so we can forget about the first three days of the week.

*****

He found the white brick Medical Arts building, a block from Soldiers Memorial. Dr. Coldwater's name was on the office directory a few names above Dr. Lang's name. It was an office just down the hall from the entrance, conveniently situated on the ground floor.

He walked past the closed door of Dr. Lang's office to Dr. Coldwater's office. The waiting room was full of mothers with young children drooling in snot, mothers holding some babies in their laps, keeping others in strollers, all crying and sneezing at the same time. The office din was making his head ache. He could smell shit and soiled diapers. He wished that he had drunk more black coffee.

He had second thoughts. Why hadn't he contacted Dr. Coldwater by phone? Dr. Coldwater's secretary looked up with an unpleasant expression on her face at his intrusion. He obviously was not a patient. In a cold voice she asked, "May I help you?"

"Dr. Eves gave me Dr. Coldwater's name. It's a murder inquiry. Dr. Coldwater was a good friend of Jerry Lang's. Does he have a few minutes between patients? I won't take long. I know his time is valuable."

"Dr. Coldwater can see you now for a few minutes in between patients. I guess they will have to wait, the patients that is. The patients should come first but in your case we can make an exception." She gave him a tight smile. She was not a gracious lady. "Take a seat, he is with someone now."

A few minutes later, Dr. Coldwater opened the door and let the mother out holding a screaming infant. He was a tall man in his late forties. Unlike Dr. Lang, he appeared to have avoided stepping into a gym all his life, a roly-poly figure, a grandfatherly presence, dressed in a white lab coat with pens and a prescription pad in his breast pocket. He had dark wavy hair with a streak of grey along the centre part.

Clancy showed his ID "I must apologize for interrupting you. I will be as quick as possible. You have heard that your friend, Dr. Lang was murdered. I am working on the case. You were a close friend and colleague of Dr. Lang."

"Come in, come in so that we can talk in private." Clancy entered his office; the walls lined with diplomas and certificates. He sat down on a chair facing a large desk. Stuffed toys were piled on the other chair.

"Shoot" said Dr. Coldwater.

"What kind of a man was Jerry Lang? Can you tell me something about him?"

"Well we went to the same high school together, London Central, He played football and was on the Golden Ghosts team. He went to Western and was on the Western football team. He was an attractive guy and had plenty of girl friends over the years. He had his pick of women. We both went to the same medical school in London, Ontario, where we graduated together. Our friendship goes back a long way."

"When did he get married?"

"He married a high school flame while in his fourth year psychiatric residency. Her father was a well-known London, doctor and she was a bright young woman. She was crazy about him. I felt sorry for her when they got divorced but that's the way things are these days."

"As a psychiatrist I bet he knew a lot of secrets about this town."

"Maybe."

"Secrets that would get him killed?"

"I don't think so. Just details about your average, every day relationships: adultery, incest, wife beating, battery and assault I don't believe that he heard confessions of murder or armed robbery," he laughed at his little joke, "this is a peaceful little town." Then he stopped smiling when he realized the irony of his comments.

"So you knew him quite well. What was his schedule like? Where did he spend most of his time?"

"He spent several days of the week over at Barrie General doing in house work, making the rounds, visiting patients that sort of thing. The rest of the week Thursday and

Friday he had private patients here in Mariposa just down the hall. Three days away and then two days here."

"Did he have any enemies? Among his colleagues? His patients?"

"He didn't express strong or controversial opinions which would offend anyone. He was likeable in a placid sort of way. He was a man of few words, didn't say much, hard to read. You got the impression that he was making mental notes and analyzing you when you were taking to him. That was the impression he gave to most people. But that was something we projected onto him, and I came to realize over time that it was just his natural expression. He smoked. He tried to break his habit not too successfully but he did cut back.

"It amazes me that doctors continue to smoke, knowing what they do. But nicotine is a powerful drug. It is supposed to be more addictive than heroin. It must be hard spending the day listening to all that stuff that he was told, I say, garbage in, and garbage out."

"He must have made someone angry enough to want to kill him."

"Seems like it."

"Did he drink?"

"On occasion, he took a social drink just like everybody else."

"Any gossip about him?"

"He kept a low profile socially, not much on the grapevine."

"I guess we'll have to dig deeper to find his enemies."

"Some patients loved him, others might not."

"What was his specialty?"

"He was an addiction counselor at the hospital and in private practice he did psychotherapy."

"Did you notice anything different in the last several months? Was there a difference in his demeanor?"

"I can't say I did. We only met passing in the hall. We never met for coffee or anything of that nature. We never met socially. He wasn't as outgoing as he was after his divorce. That's about all I can tell you." Dr. Coldwater lifted up a file. "Got to get back to work and deal with the little buggers."

"Thanks for your time." Then Clancy got up and walked back through the howling din of the waiting room. Well that interview hadn't been too enlightening thought Clancy. So far no suspects. I'll have to dig deeper.

* * * * *

The old red brick building of the RBC branch, built at the turn of the century was located on the corner across from the Opera House. Clancy thought he would nip in and see whether Dr. Lang's finances were in order. That might give him a clue or a direction to take. Near the bank's glass revolving doors a *Help yourself* sign sat on a bridge table, holding a silver canister of coffee, with paper cups, cookies, milk, sugar, stirrers placed next to it. Clancy could never resist a doughnut. He bent down and picked up a maple coated doughnut which he wrapped in a paper napkin to eat later. His fingers felt sticky and now was not the time to wipe them on anything.

A voice at his elbow boomed, "May I help you?" Clancy gave a start. He hadn't seen the man standing next to the coffee table. It was the floor manager waiting to direct him to a teller or to business accounts.

"I'm here in a professional capacity." His hand quickly hid the doughnut behind his back. "I came to see about a client."

"Then you will want to speak to our Branch Manager. This way." He ushered Clancy towards a glass enclosed air conditioned room at one end of the building.

Clancy knocked on the glass window of the door. A loud voice boomed from within, "Enter."

The Bank Manager who had been cleaning his fingernails, hastily slipped the file into the drawer and closed it. He was a short pudgy middle aged man dressed in a dark navy business suit who had gotten used to dealing with clients who pleaded *can I borrow*, and *I need*.... One dead beat off the street had come in for a loan. During the brief interview, his trousers had fallen to his ankles.

Clancy flashed his ID. "I am here to see about Dr. Lang's accounts."

"Give me a few minutes so I can pull up his accounts on my computer. Dreadful business isn't it? I heard about it on the radio. Dr. Lang was a good customer of ours. I was well acquainted with him. He had just taken out a second mortgage on that big house of his. He had to take out a line of credit to pay for his new car, a nice one, a Lexus."

"What were his finances like?"

"To all appearances, Dr. Lang was a successful doctor but it might surprise many that he was barely meeting his payments. Appearances are very deceiving. People see a big house on the hill and a flashy new car, but they don't ask. Is it paid for? A lot of professionals are maxed out. Jerry Lang, if you want my opinion lived close to the wire. Does that help?"

"Well at least it fills in a blank."

"A lot of people who live by Lake Couchiching in big houses appear to have money. It's a façade, they are mortgaged to the eyeballs. Don't believe all that you see. There are a lot of phonies out there."

"Did Dr. Lang act stressed about his financial debt? Anxious?"

"No, he just said, I have a huge load on my back and it would be nice to see the end of it."

"Were there any big withdrawals during the last six months, any unusual cash withdrawals?"

"Not that I can see. He had the usual deposits at the beginning of the month, then the payments, and charges later. Nothing out of the ordinary. Here take a look for yourself."

Clancy looked at the screen. "Nothing seemed unusual. Thanks," said Clancy getting up to leave. "Oh my gawd." He had sat down on his doughnut and it was now sticking to the wedge in the seat of his trousers. As delicately as he could he reached behind and pinched the doughnut, "I must have sat on something. I need a Kleenex."

"Here," said the manager, his eyes bulging.

Clancy then slipped the sugary mess into it which he dropped into the waste basket on his way out.

* * * * *

The heat had been oppressive, which was rare for June. There was a strong wind blowing all morning. It was strong enough to blow away lawn chairs rattle the deck awnings and rip up the outdoor real estate signs. The winds were approaching 100 miles an hour, a dangerous wind storm to be out in with swirling leaves and debris of sticks, stones and branches being swept about.

David listened to the news and the latest weather report. A dark funnel cloud, a tornado had touched down twice on the horizon outside Mariposa. He waited for the follow up. There was no damage just a strong wind blowing things about. "Isn't that amazing, no damage to the houses, to the barns, to the fences, and no injuries. It's a miracle."

"I guess the good people were on their knees praying," added Clancy. "Usually tornados do a hell of a lot of damage."

"Were you praying, Clancy?"

"I'm not the praying kind" said Clancy sounding irritated." I have a lot of important things to do like interviews."

Clancy had gotten the first Mrs. Evelyn Lang's phone number in London, Ontario from Brenda. He decided to find out what she had to say about her ex-husband.

"Hello, hello." the line had gone dead. I will call again. He went back to filling out a report on the investigation so far for Bob White. He tried again a couple of more times. When the report was finished he rang again. A cultured woman's voice answered the phone. "Is this Mrs. Lang? It's Detective Clancy Murphy of the Mariposa OPP. I am investigating the murder of your ex-husband."

"I'm still in shock."

"How did you first learn about it?"

"I saw it in the Globe and Mail obituaries. I can't get over it."

"I wonder if you could give me a picture of what he was like as a person. Do you have a few minutes?"

"Well we have been separated for five years and divorced for three, so my impressions will be a little bit dated."

"Anything will help."

"Well Jerry was a deeply private person, very closed off. You didn't quite know where you stood with him because he never revealed his feelings. He made a good bridge player because you never knew what cards he held in his hands. But lack of intimacy was a problem. Even though he was a therapist and knew how important intimacy was, he never confided his deepest feelings. He was a deep person, very quiet and hardly said a thing. He let me make all the major decisions like buying the house, arranging for the vacations etc. Whatever you want to do, I trust your judgment, he said."

"Did you ever fight at all?"

"No, and the reason was because he didn't show his anger, his emotions. He'd go for a jog. Maybe that was how he got rid of his aggression. We never fought which should have been a warning sign in the relationship.

I never realized that he was unhappy or wanted a change until he came home one day, asking for a divorce, just out of the blue."

"He wanted the divorce?"

"Yes, out of the blue. I had no warning."

"I asked him to go for marriage counseling which we did. He went reluctantly. "Since when did a psychiatrist go for marriage counseling?" he said He considered it a waste of time. I was up against a stone wall. I asked him if there was another woman. He denied it and said no. There usually is.

"He lied. He had another woman, a nurse whom he subsequently married, a little sexpot who couldn't keep her hands off him. I had no chance to save the marriage.

"I have moved on. At least I am not one of those wives that sacrifice everything financially to put her husband through medical school and then get dumped."

"When was the last time you saw him?"

"I haven't seen him in three years since our divorce. That was in October of that year."

"Have you any idea of anyone who would want to kill him?"

"No one, unless it was a patient with violent tendencies. It's a shame."

"Well thank you, Mrs. Lang and I may need to contact you again while the investigation is continuing."

"I don't know what further help I can be."

"Well if I need you I will call but in the meantime, there is a lot of ground to cover."

* * * * *

"I wonder when Dr. Lang's funeral will take place?" asked Greg.

"As soon as the body is released to the next of kin, the funeral can be arranged. He picked up the Mariposa News which was lying on a table. "Here it is, the announcement states that the funeral will be held Saturday June 26th at Mariposa United Church at 1 pm. That's the red brick church on Peter St., on the corner, opposite the Anglican Church. Up the street is the Presbyterian Church whose church bells never seem to be inactive. There are no excuses for the locals not to go to church."

"That's today. We should go and keep our eyes open, particularly on the mourners. Our murderer might be among the mourners." suggested Clancy. "I'll take David. Greg you can mind the store."

"Thanks heaps," replied Greg.

The weather had changed. Mists were coming in off the lake, leaving the park and the marina in fog so thick that the fir trees were just grey shadows. It was eerie how the fog and mist cloaked everything. The humidity didn't let up. It was a hot afternoon. Too hot for a funeral. It was all very depressing. Then it began to rain, a cooling spring rain. Clancy could hear the patter on the roof of the church. But then it quickly cleared up again.

With five minutes to go before the service started, they entered the church's side door. After taking the program from the usher, they slipped into a rear pew at the back of the church as unobtrusively as possible which was a bit difficult since they both were wearing their uniforms and stood out like sore thumbs.

Huge bouquets of white calla lilies banked the front of the church, on both sides of the main aisle below the altar. The smell of the lilies was too sweet almost sickening. Thankfully the lower half of the stained glass windows had been opened so that the mourners could get a cooling breeze.

The organist began playing the funeral march. On cue the pallbearers in mourning suits, with black arm bands and white gloves brought the expensive bronze casket up the steps through the open church door into the sanctuary. The casket on casters was rolled down the main aisle to the altar.

Entering the church last, making a grand entrance, was the tearful widow Mrs. Brenda Lang. She looked very fetching, wearing a black lace dress and a black broad brimmed hat framing her long blond hair. She was escorted to the front pew leaning heavily on the arm of Dr. Coldwater, Dr. Lang's closest friend. That's interesting, thought Clancy, how chummy those two are. On the other hand, Dr. Coldwater might be making some remarks during the service and he needed to sit near the front of the church.

The official mourners mostly men, dressed in black mourning suits followed her up the aisle falling back to sit in the seats reserved for them behind Mrs. Lang's pew. Most of the professional community in Mariposa had shown up. Clancy recognized a couple of judges from Barrie, several lawyers from a downtown law firm, and the rest he guessed were doctors, colleagues of Dr. Lang. He recognized Dr. Frost, the coroner. Some were from the hospital in Barrie, others from Soldiers Memorial. His patients, no doubt were scattered amongst the many mourners throughout the church.

Reverend Day in his white robes with trailing green banners left his chair in the pulpit to come and stand in front of the congregation. "We are here today to celebrate the life of Dr. Lang who was brutally murdered. Even though Dr. Lang lived in Mariposa for less than ten years he made a valuable contribution to the community. He made a remarkable impression on everyone he met.

"We value life. We are all special in the eyes of God. Dr. Lang was special."

The hymn, *Abide with me* was sung. After the hymn finished, they sat down, Dr. Coldwater left the front pew, walked up the chancel steps and stood in the pulpit to give the eulogy mentioning the fact that their friendship went way back to medical school in London, Ontario. Dr. Lang was passionate about running, good health and keeping fit. In his professional life, Dr. Lang never turned a patient away that he thought he could help. He would live on through the hearts of his patients."

It was a very well done tribute and said in a positive way, despite the gruesomeness of Dr. Lang being murdered. Clancy was impressed.

The last prayers were said; a blessing for the eternal soul of Dr. Lang and then the pallbearers with heads bowed came forward and wheeled the casket down the aisle. Brenda Lang followed with loud sobbing. Dr. Coldwater had a tight grip on her arm, as he partly walked, partly dragged her behind the casket. It was not a dignified sight.

"Where will the remains be buried? Should we go out to the cemetery?" asked David.

"It says here, in the announcements and order of service, that it there will be a cremation followed by private internment to be attended by family members only. That leaves us out. It would take a lot of nerve to crash that, even if we stood at the rear of the cemetery. Well that's that. I didn't see much of anything of interest. Nothing that I could put my finger on. Did you, David?" Clancy stood up to go, nodding at several mourners who passed him on the aisle.

"No it may have been a complete waste of time for all we know. You do a lot of things in this job, that are a complete waste of time."

"Back to the office and see if Greg has got any incoming calls on witnesses to the Trans Canada Trail."

"I doubt it. Friday afternoon people are getting ready for the cottage, not thinking about jogging, shopping for groceries, getting the car tanked up, that sort of thing. I am not surprised if we don't hear anything. It's early days yet. We will keep the posters up hoping it jogs somebody's memory."

* * * * *

Once the funeral was over, the next thing on the agenda was to speak to Dr. Lang's nurse. He drove over to the Medical

Arts Building on Mississauga West, circled the parking lot several times and eventually found a parking spot. He found Dr. Lang's office number posted on the directory inside the door. Suite 200. He buzzed. He buzzed again. On the third buzz, a click and then a soft gentle voice answered, "Yes?"

"Police," he said. She buzzed him in.

He walked along the carpeted hall and found Dr. Lang's office two doors from the end of the hall opposite the Men's Washroom. Suite 200, He knocked and finding the door unlocked, let himself in.

In a corner of the empty waiting room was the receptionist with a sign on her desk reading, "**Nurse Amy Sweet**." A good looking blonde with shoulder length hair stared at him. Her pale blue eyes were blood shot from weeping. She had the most woebegone, expression on her face.

He flashed his ID.

"I need your help in finding Dr. Lang's killer," he said. "Anything you can tell me will help."

"I will be glad to help in any way possible."

"Can you give me a list of patients with their phone numbers? We will have to review case by case, going by the notes that Dr. Lang wrote after he saw each patient. Can you also give me his day appointment book? I want to pay attention to the patients he saw on his last day and his activities for that day, June 19th, and also for the preceding day."

She blinked up at him. "Health records are confidential."

"Not in a murder inquiry, they are not."

"I'll do the best I can. I can't think of anyone that would want to kill Dr. Lang. He was such a kind man. He was the nicest man to work for."

"Can you think of any patient? Does any patient stand out as violent? Abusive? Controlling? Can you think of any patient that would want to kill him?"

"Except for the depressives, most patients had a little bit of both, depression and anger. They all had their problems. But off hand I can't think of one that stands out as being violent."

"Has any patient ever threatened him? Have you heard

of a patient shouting at him? Remonstrating with him? Ever tried to blackmail him?"

"I will have to give it some thought."

"How long have you worked for Dr. Lang?"

"For the past three years."

"Have you had any break-ins? Any attempt to steal cash or drugs?"

"Yes, but it was a small amount. Now we don't keep any drugs on the premises."

"If I can see the files for the patients he had on his last three days it might be a good place to start. There's a lot of work to cover. "

"I'll get them for you." She got up from her chair and went over to the filing cabinet, to look them up and then gave them to him. "I have given you the files of patients who saw him those last days. I have also given you from the computer list of all the patients' names and contact information. If that can be of any help?"

"Thank you I will need more information as the investigation progresses."

"I'll do anything I can to help you. Dr. Lang didn't deserve this." She sat down at her desk again holding a handkerchief up to her eyes.

"Thanks, Miss Sweet. Dr. Lang went home after his last session to pick up his sports gear. Or did he go straight to the jogging trail? What time did he usually go jogging?"

"Around 4.30. But I can't state that as a fact as he usually leaves here after 3.30. I always leave at 4 so I can't tell you for sure whether he went home or not."

"Thanks. I may need your help again."

"If I am not here, you can find me at home trying to find another job or taking a break having a coffee at Apple Annie's."

He tipped his hat. It was always a pleasure to talk to a beautiful young nurse like Miss Sweet who seemed so unaware of her charms. Too bad that he was a married man, otherwise things might be different.

* * * * *

Back in the office, Clancy had settled himself at his desk for only a few minutes before his office door flew open with a bang. What a nerve! There was Mira, the newspaper journalist from the Mariposa News Packet wearing a tight white T-shirt covering her bouncing breasts and a black leather mini skirt, with her notebook clasped to her bosom. Not waiting for an invitation to come in, she strode into the room and plopped herself down in a chair facing him .There was nothing shy about Mira. "How's the investigation going Clancy? Any suspects so far?"

"My, my Mira but you're coming on strong. It's early days yet, Mira. We are at the preliminary stages of weeding out the suspects and eliminating those that don't fit."

"Well, give me a hint of what direction you are going in?"

"One of the problems is nice Dr. Lang had no known enemies. He was to all appearances a nice guy. It is hard to find anyone that had a grudge against him, or a motive to kill him."

"What about his patients? He must have been treating a few violent ones?"

"So far nothing yet."

Mira slammed her notebook down on his desk. "People in Mariposa are nervous with a killer walking loose amongst us. Old ladies aren't getting much sleep at night, along with the rest of us. That includes me. What are you doing to calm their fears?"

At which Clancy rolled his eyes.

"Not getting enough sleep, Mira? There can be many reasons for that, not just a murderer loose." He raised one eyebrow and paused.

Mira returned the stare.

"Mira, we are doing the best we can. We are working flat out interviewing potential suspects. Other than that I don't know what more we can do."

"Well come up with something soon or people will begin to think that the police aren't making an effort, that they aren't up to scratch."

"We're working flat out. Mira. I wish I could be more

helpful."

"Remember no news is not good news. "Mira slammed her notebook down on his desk and got up from her chair.

"And your job is to sell newspapers." said Clancy as Mira stormed out of the door. He turned to David who had his head down amongst some papers pretending not to have heard anything. "David, your old pal was just in, she wasn't very friendly. I guess you pissed her off but good."

"One man alone can't satisfy Mira."

"Uh, I see. So that's the way it is. We're in deep freeze territory, are we? Well try to get the situation unfrozen. We need all the help we can get. Mira could be very helpful."

* * * * *

Not waiting for another interruption, Clancy began reading through the patient's files, flipping through the manila folders. There was a lot to cover and quite a few people to interview. After an hour he took a break. He went over to David's desk and put his hand on his shoulder.

"How did your camping weekend go?"

"Not bad. We canoed on Canoe Lake, portaged, and did some swimming. Algonquin Park is pretty popular with other campers though. We did some hiking nothing too strenuous. At night we found a spot out in the open, pitched our tent and put our food way up in a tree so that the bears couldn't get at it. We built a camp fire. Food cooked outdoors always tastes good. First night we had pork chops with corn on the cob. The second night we had steak with baked potatoes. Chipmunks scampered out of the woods and gathered around us while we ate. Later in the dark, we could hear the shrill cry of the loon coming across the lake. Our pup tent, though, was a little small. It was hard to roll over."

"I bet it was. Hard to turn over, eh? Did you see any wildlife?"

"When we were paddling, I saw a bull moose swimming along the edge of the lake near the shore. When we got closer, he took off. Got some nasty mosquito bites on the bum from peeing outdoors. But you can't do anything about that."

"That's something. Now get back to work, David, my boy. It's time to rise and shine. You need a little exercise and more fresh air. We are at early days in the investigation but now we are going to interview potential suspects. I've found a sensitive soul, a patient of Dr. Lang's for you to interview. Proceed delicately. Don't push him over the edge or give him another nervous breakdown, judging from what is written in Dr. Lang's file. We don't want a police harassment charge filed against us.

"Miss Sweet, Dr. Lang's secretary gave me his name, one of his patients whom Dr. Lang saw on one of his last days. Nip over and see what he has to say."

"He sounds like a boring old geezer that you want to unload on me. If he was a challenge you would go there yourself."

"Don't be so suspicious, David. I have only your best interests at heart."

"Yeh, sure."

David found his address on file and drove over. Mr. Small lived on Brant Street in an old two story Victorian house, which looked neglected judging by the tall uncut grass on the front lawn full of weeds The house needed painting and the trim in places was worn away The drain pipes were snapped off at the corners. The hedge in front of the house blocking the view from the windows hadn't been clipped in years, its branches reaching out in all directions. Cracks in the pavement broke up the sidewalk. David found the front door in the alcove off the veranda and rang the bell.

When the door opened. A thin little man in a dressing gown, trousers and bedroom slippers peered out at him. It looked like Mr. Small's eyes were red from crying.

"May I come in? Mr. Small? I have your name from the files as being a patient of Dr. Lang's. You had an appointment with him on that last Friday, 13th."

"If I can help. Terrible business. Just terrible. Come back to the kitchen. That is where I usually sit in the mornings reading the paper, having a cup of tea or just looking out the window. It's along this passage way."

David followed him along a dreary hall, with faded wall

paper, one bare light bulb hung from the ceiling and piles of old newspaper were stashed in one corner.

I don't know what to do now that Dr. Lang is gone. There are only a few psychiatrists in Mariposa. They all have a long waiting list. I don't know if I can get a replacement. I don't know how I am going to get my medication."

He sniffed and blew his nose into a large grey cotton handkerchief that he pulled from his back pocket. It looked filthy.

There were stacks of dirty dishes in the sink and on the countertop. By way of explanation, Mr. Small said, "My wife has left me and I have had to cope on my own. I am not doing a good job of coping."

David swept the old newspapers off a chair and sat down, hoping that the chair was clean enough to sit down on. 'I am here in the hope that you can give me some insight into who might have murdered Dr. Lang. "What did you see him about? How long have you been going to see him?'

"Off and on for over three years ever since I lost my job. I can barely meet the mortgage payments on this house. Financially things aren't good. I have been on unemployment insurance and then that ran out and at the same time, my wife left. No money, no honey. That's the way the world turns."

"How did Dr. Lang appear to you as a person? Or was he just a professional in a white coat to you?"

"He was very kind man, very gentle. But the last day I found him a bit tense. He seemed unhappy. Because of my depression I usually can spot someone in the same mood as myself. He just wasn't up if you know what I mean."

"Did he allude to it in any way? Make a comment or something?"

"Nothing."

"Have you any idea who might want to kill him?"

"No one. I can't think of any reason for someone to do that. We all needed him."

"What did he prescribe for you?"

"Tranquilizers, Valium to be specific. Enough for three months, so I don't run out of it. I can't tell you much more than that."

"If you think of anything, let me know." David handed him his card.

"I will. Can you find your way out?"

David retraced his steps down the hall and then shut the front door. Well I don't think he is the one, too depressed to act on his emotions. He would turn inward, to self-hating. In my opinion he is a real sad sack. We could interview half of Mariposa and get no further ahead. Obviously his patients in Barrie would not know that he went jogging after work every day so we can forget about the first three days of the week that he saw patients in Barrie unless something develops. Some of the patients he saw like Mr. Small are depressives and unless they have a reason to flip out, I can't see them doing anything.

It was a complete waste of time. But in a murder investigation, a lot of trails lead nowhere but they still have to be pursued.

* * * * *

Clancy looked up from his desk over at Greg who was trying to look busy but not succeeding. "Greg, you don't seem to have much on your plate. There were no break and enters last night. Pop around to Dunkin Donuts and get some sugary ones which we can have with our afternoon coffee."

"Are you treating?"

"Dutch treat."

"I get to do all the dirty work."

"You're out in the fresh air. It's good for you. It's a beautiful spring day. The robins are out getting worms and that is what we should be doing."

David looked up from his desk. "That old geezer, Mr. Small, that you sent me to interview looked and acted so depressed that I felt sorry for him. He seemed too depressed to kill a mouse. It was a waste of time."

"We have to interview all kinds, just to make sure we don't arrest the wrong person. We don't want to be accused by the Crown of having tunnel vision when we come to make an arrest. Who was the last patient to see Dr. Lang that day? I'll phone Nurse Sweet and double check." Clancy picked up the phone and punched in the numbers.

"She says she was just going on her break and it was lucky I caught her. She says it was Eric Badas, a local fireman. In his file it says he came to Dr. Lang for solutions in anger management. He might prove worth interviewing. He has an interesting background. He was up on an assault and battery charge recently."

"It sounds as if that person is a good possibility," said David.

"Listen to this. One night in an alcoholic stupor, he brutally beat his wife black and blue. Part of his sentence was that he had to take an anger management course in counseling. By doing so many days of community service, and doing counseling, he could keep his job as a fireman and have no criminal record. What if he had lost control again?"

'"We have to find a motive in that case. I can assume that I can find him at the local fire hall on Mississauga, the main street."

"Yes, he works out of there. He might be on shift work but that's his local."

David didn't need to drive; it was just a short walk to the fire station. The large front doors were open. Out front one of the fire men in rubber boots and long rubber pants held up by suspenders was using the fire hose to wash down the front of the fire truck.

"Where can I find Mr.Badas?"

"He is probably playing cards upstairs with the rest of the men.

"Walk in and take the stairs on your left."

Climbing the stairs David found four men sitting at a card table intently looking at their cards.

"Mr. Badas?"

A man with a handlebar mustache and sideburns jerked around and looked up. "Yes?"

"I would like to talk to you on a private matter. Sorry to interrupt your game."

"I bet you are," his voice was heavy with sarcasm. Annoyed, he threw down his cards on the table. "Just when I was winning. It always happens, just when I have a good hand.

I hope it's important enough to interrupt my game?"

"It will only take a few minutes. Is there an office or private room in the back?"

"Yeh, in the back where we get our forty winks when not on call. It's called the sleep room." Eric led him back to the room and flicked on the light. The walls were papered with calendars of busty dames in bikinis picking up weights. A brew master pot with coffee cups sat on a ledge. A couch with a pillow and a grey blanket for napping was pressed against one wall. Two chairs sat off to one side and a small bridge table. Eric indicated for David to sit down.

"What's this about? This is not a social call, I gather. I don't appreciate the OPP coming here to snoop around at my place of work. A phone call would be more discreet and I could arrange to meet you outside my place of work. This is kind of embarrassing. My work mates will wonder why you are here. What is this all about?"

"Your therapist got wacked and you were one of the last persons to see him alive. I want your impressions or your last appointment in his office."

"I heard something about this on the radio. When did this happen?"

"Friday. He was out jogging on the Trans Canada Trail and someone stabbed him in the back."

"It's hard to believe. I know nothing about this, just what I read in the newspaper and heard on the radio."

"Where were you on Friday 13th...except for your appointment with Dr. Lang?"

"I was on duty here at the station."

"The whole time?"

"The guys on the staff will vouch for me. Besides I signed in on the time sheet."

"Any breaks?"

"Half hour in the afternoon."

"Where?"

"I can't recall exactly."

"Try to remember."

"Can't. Busy afternoon"

David changed tack. "How long have you been seeing

Dr. Lang?"

"Six months or so."

"How is it progressing?"

"Takes time. Rome wasn't built in a day. My probation will soon be up."

"Glad to hear it. Take me back to that last day. Was Dr. Lang any different do you recall, than he usually was? Can you describe him for me?"

"Well I went into his office, and took a seat. He asked me to tell him how my life was going since I had last seen him. I had been practicing the technique of counting to ten before blowing off. I have tried to avoid situations that I recognize will set me off. I have cut back on my drinking."

"Dr. Lang's demeanor?"

"He was hard to read. That day he seemed a little more tense, His eyes were wandering around the room then looking out the window. He wasn't focused on what I was saying. He wasn't listening. I had to repeat something that I had already told him and he hadn't remembered. He just wasn't concentrating. This was irritating to me. You'd like to think that your shrink is listening to what you are telling him."

"Did he say anything at all?"

"No, only he cut the session short by ten minutes. He was in a rush to get away."

"Mm."

"Does that help?"

"Not much." David picked up his jacket ready to go. "Don't spend your time looking at these dames, Eric, you'll go blind." He chuckled.

"I can dream, can't I? My old lady is on the heavy side. It's a shame about Dr. Lang."

"Everyone seems to think so. I'll find my way out."

* * * * *

While David was out interviewing Badas, Clancy looked at the files again. There was another name, another suspect to interview. He called the number that was listed. The line was busy. He waited a few minutes and then he called again. A woman with a deep husky voice answered.

"Yes, how can I help you?"

"Mrs. Holly Jones? I got your name from Dr. Lang's office. You were one of the last patients to see him alive the day he was murdered. I would like to come by and talk to you and get your help in our inquiries. Will you be in later this morning?"

"Well yes, I will be. I was going to go out and do some shopping but I will stay in and wait for you to come by. I hope it won't take long. I have an appointment with my trainer at noon."

Clancy found the Jones house, in a posh section of Mariposa, a large rectangular one level ranch style bungalow at the end of a cull de sac that led down to the lake with a fenced-in pool to the side of the house. Seeing the pool Clancy made him a little envious. Why can't they swim in the lake? Isn't the lake good enough for them? They probably also have a hot tub on the pool's deck.

He knocked once, then he gave the oak door a good rap. He noticed the security camera above the door.

A tall, slim, well-tanned woman, a brunette in her late thirties or early forties, but she could easily pass for much younger answered the door. "Come in. I have been expecting you. My husband, Hugh is at work in Barrie and there is just little old me in the house. It can get lonely sometimes."

Clancy flashed his ID. "I am calling concerning Dr. Lang, This is a murder investigation."

"Yes, I understand. How dreadful. Come into the lounge and sit down. Make yourself comfortable." Clancy glanced around the room. The sofa and stuffed chairs were from the Bombay Company. He had been admiring the pieces on display in the store window but they were much too grand for his pocket book. Mrs. Jones slipped into a chair opposite him crossed and uncrossed her long slim legs. Her red painted fingernails flashed as she opened a package of cigarettes that she took out of her leather purse. "I hope you don't mind my smoking. It calms the nerves. Do you have a light?"

Clancy fished into his back pocket and came up with a lighter. He flipped it open and gave it to her.

"Thanks." She paused and blew a smoke ring into the air. She looked poised, sleek and well-coiffed. She didn't look nervous at all about being interviewed by the police. He could feel a certain sexual tension in the air.

"How long have you been seeing Dr. Lang?"

"I have been seeing him for over two years. The next question you will ask is why. I have to tell you why because you will find out soon enough that I have a prior record or in your terminology a rap sheet. You see I am a kleptomaniac." She sounded like she was telling him she had a PhD and was proud of it. "Part of my conditional sentence is that I must seek counseling." She tapped his knee with her hand.

"I have this compulsion, you see, to go shopping and to boost objects while I am at it."

"Where do you steal?"

"Not here in Mariposa, over in Barrie. One does not want to muddy one's own nest. I drive over to Barrie, I wear a long sleeve jacket or coat and carry a carry all for boosting. Then while browsing before I know it, something has landed in my bag. I don't even recall picking it up. I just see something and then it's bang. It's gone. It's stuff I don't need or want. I just have these urges to go and do this. I am good at it. I have only been caught a couple of times. Sometimes the security guard has caught me in the act. Then he takes me back to the office where I meet the store manager. Then, he calls my husband. My husband, pleads with him, and says I am a sick woman and then offers to pay. I take out my cheque book and write a cheque, Often I am carrying enough cash to pay for the items. Cash is better. It leaves no paper trail. I sign a document about what I have done. It is dated and witnessed. Then I am escorted out of the store and told never to come back again. I will soon be running out of stores to shop in.

The last time, despite my pleas and tears not to call the police, they did. I was arrested. The police wrote it up. I went before a judge. I received a suspended sentence. I have to do so many hours of community service and to seek counseling. It is so embarrassing but it does not stop the compulsion. I have to learn what sets it off. To foresee the danger, the signs before it happens."

"Here's a warning sign. I'll book you if I ever catch you stealing in front of me in Mariposa. No problem. What about your husband? What does he think about all this?"

She shrugged her shoulders. "Hugh is very forgiving and very supportive. I feel I don't deserve his love for all that he has to put up with. I am ashamed of what I do. Deeply ashamed." She lowered her head and turned her face away from him. But somehow to Clancy her shame rang hollow. She got off on doing it and would have continued to do it if she hadn't got caught.

"Are you ashamed enough to quit?" Clancy let the question hang in the air. She didn't answer but look down at her feet. "Getting back to Dr. Lang. Have you any thoughts about that last morning? Do you recall your last session with him?"

"Not really. He just said the usual preamble. 'Tell me what has been going on in your life since I last saw you and to continue from there. After that session which lasted 50 minutes he went home for lunch."

"Nothing unusual or anything out of the ordinary?"

"No, He just seemed to be a little rushed to get home for lunch, that's all."

"Thank you. If I have any more questions, I will get hold of you. Where were you on June 19th around 4.30 pm?"

"I can't remember. Either at home or grocery shopping. I like to swim in the afternoons. I have no alibi. Am I a suspect?" She grabbed his knee tightly. He backed away from her.

"Every patient is a suspect until we eliminate everyone except the murderer."

"I hope I am not being framed for this because my husband and I will fight every inch of the way. I have the claws of a tiger. I won't take this sitting down."

"I'm sure you have."

Clancy got back into his car and was almost back at the office when he realized he was missing something. Damn, she had boosted his lighter. Well the next time he interviewed her he would get it back.

* * * * *

It was another glorious summer day, not too hot, or humid, just right. For exercise and he did need some, Clancy sauntered down the street whistling and tipping his hat to two old ladies who smiled at him as he walked by. He entered the Dead Tired Pool Hall. Chances are 100 to one, that little weasel, Jimmy Snipe would be found here. It was his home away from home. He wanted to have a chat. Why would that drug pusher see a psychiatrist? Was the relationship mutually beneficial between the supplier and the addict?

The windowless room was in gloom except for the few players at the pool table their faces lit up by the light of the pool table lamp. A few stragglers were sitting at nearby tables nursing a beer, and drowning their sorrows. Jimmy was leaning against the back wall watching the players.

"Jimmy, may I have a word? I am investigating the murder of your psychiatrist, Dr. Lang."

"Well I had nothing to do with it. Don't bother me."

"You were one of the last people to see him alive."

"I was just in and out of his office in fifteen minutes."

"Yeah. What were you seeing him for?"

"My bad back."

"Your bad back? My, my. When did you get that?"

"I was working at the liquor store and a case of beer fell off the trolley onto my lower back and injured my spinal cord and the surrounding muscles."

"And how does a psychiatrist treat a bad back?" sneered Clancy

"I went to him for his help in managing my pain. The treatment is called pain management."

"Oh my what big words we're using. Who suggested that?"

"Workman's Compensation Board. They are paying. I have incredible back pain."

"I bet you have."

"And what did the good doctor prescribe for you? OxyNeo? Am I right? And you being a good boy are taking it? I don't even bother to ask."

"Off my case, will you."

"I am not interested in OxyNeo at the moment I just

want to hear your impressions of Dr. Lang that day."

A small sign of relief escaped from Snipe's lips. "Well he was a bit rushed. In a hurry, he had two more patients to see after me. I asked for the prescription. He gave it to me and I thanked him. He was preoccupied. He just was not paying too much attention to me. On the other hand, I had come in and asked him for a favour and I was interrupting his schedule."

"Just like that, huh? We'll be in touch. Don't wander too far. Think it over and see if you can come up with something interesting." Clancy headed back to the office.

"Any luck?" asked David.

"The interview gives me a little insight but not much. But this is early days yet."

"What's on tap for tonight?"

"There's nothing much on the agenda. I expect a quiet evening. Go home and see how my dog, Mike is. Let him out for a run in the backyard. Then I will turn on the lawn sprinklers. Put water in the bird bath. I have had to grease the bird feeder pole. The squirrels are always trying to climb up it. Then do a little weeding in the rose garden, sprinkle some fertilizer. Roses need a lot of fertilizer. Hope it is quiet on the lake and there are no intoxicated boaters out there that we have to go out and fine."

"Well I have no lawn to cut, one of the advantages of living in an apartment but maybe I'll drive by the lake and catch the cooling breezes. There is always someone fishing on the dock or kayaking on the lake. See you tomorrow."

* * * * *

Another nice sunny spring day, but Clancy found it hard to concentrate on catching the murderer with his dog Mike so ill. He pushed the files on his desk aside. He felt depressed. "I have got to take my dog, Mike to the vet. Mike is not getting any better. The vet is going to charge me a bomb. I'm off there and then when I come back, I will interview another suspect."

"When you love something, it doesn't matter how much

it will cost," piped up Greg.

"You can say that. But it is not you that's paying."

In the car, it was hard to look at his dog so quiet with its head down tucked into the blankets, so unlike its usual energetic self, standing at the car's window sniffing the air and barking.

He carried the dog in and handed the dog over to the vet. "Bye Mike," and he buried his face in his fur. Mike looked so sad, holding its head in its paws.

But it had to be done.

To take his mind off his dog, he set out to interview another of Dr. Lang's patients, Adam Fair, who was working in Mariposa Blooms Flower Shop on Mississauga. Opening the door set off a tinkling of chimes. Clancy waited for someone to come out of the back room. The smell of flowers, their sweetness was overpowering, the same cloying smell he found at a funeral home. A skinny young man in jeans and black skull and cross bone T-shirt with a Mohawk haircut and a gold earring in one ear came out of the back. He had been putting vases of red roses in the walk-in refrigerator. A nice little faggie, thought Clancy, as the youth minced his way towards him. But he on the other hand must think the police were pigs.

Clancy showed him his ID and asked to speak to Adam Fair.

"That's me. What do you want? I haven't done anything," giving him a sullen look.

"Who says you have? I am conducting a murder inquiry concerning the death of Dr. Lang."

"Yes, I heard. Sorry to hear that."

"How long have you been a patient of Dr. Lang's?"

"For several years."

"May I ask the reason why? This conversation is confidential, just between you and me." Clancy winked.

"Oh sure, trust the fuzz? That is a new one." He laughed bitterly. "But I haven't got much choice, have I? You're here and things will go easier I assume if I co-operate." He put his hands on his hip and took a deep breath. "Here goes. I came to Dr. Lang in my late teens, because of my shame about being gay." He glanced up at Clancy's face to see what effect his remark was making on him but Clancy's face was a blank. "It is very hard to come out in a small community such as Mariposa. I had told several friends in high school but had not come out publicly."

"How often did you see him?" asked Clancy brusquely.

"At least every two weeks and then it became every three weeks."

"What did you talk about?"

"We talked about gender, feelings. Sometimes I wanted to be a woman, to dress like a woman, to act like a woman."

"Huh? Go slower, pal, so that I can understand what you are saying. Gender feelings? What does that mean?"

"Okay. For me it is a state of mind sometimes very fluid. Sometimes I feel masculine and other times I feel feminine. How was I going to resolve the issue that at times I felt masculine and other times I felt feminine in one body?"

"Huh? You lost me there."

"Sometimes there is a place where the feelings meet, other times the place is in between."

"Mm. That takes a little stretch to understand and I am trying hard to," said Clancy. "When do you express your feminine side?"

"On the weekends, I escape to Boys Town in Toronto, to the gay district. I put on makeup, glue on my false eyelashes, sometimes wear a wig, padded underwear in all the right places and slip into a dress and strut my stuff up and down Church Street."

"Red high heels and feathers eh?"

"Yes. I don't get sneering cat calls, like sissy, pansy etc. which I would if I did that here in Mariposa. It is very liberating. I thought of being a drag queen. But I am not ready for it yet. I wear my outfit all weekend and I feel good as a woman. But I know it is all fake and then like Cinderella, at the end of the weekend, I take it off, wash my cosmetics off and then pack my clothes in my suitcase and board the Greyhound to come home, I can't do it in Mariposa, that is for sure."

"True, you might get your ass busted for causing a disturbance and breaking the peace of this nice little town. What treatment did Dr. Lang suggest? What kind of medication?"

"Well when I first came to see him, I was on tranquilizers for bad nerves. I was very unhappy, almost suicidal but after a couple years of therapy, I could stop taking them. Now since my objective is to be a trainwoman, he prescribed testosterone blockers and estrogen. Estrogen is making my body softer and wider in the right places. I am going to keep my penis, though."

"Lucky you, keeping your dick. How long have you been on estrogen?" He couldn't see a big change in this youth before him. He appeared androgynous yes, but anything else, no."

"Not that long."

"So you come to the good doc and you tell him all your troubles. So it was all hunky dory between you and the doctor?"

"That's about right."

"So you liked Dr. Lang?"

"Well, I didn't dislike him. He was helping me."

"He was killed on June 19. "You had an appointment with him that day. The third last appointment of the day."

"Yes."

"What was he like to you on that day?"

"The same as always. He made notes in my file."

"Was anything unusual or out of place? Did you notice anything?"

"He was not paying as much attention. It was a warm afternoon and I thought that the good weather was making him restless. It's going to be hard for me to find a psychiatrist who is as sympathetic as he was. It took me a year to find Dr. Lang and I need someone to fill my prescription if I am going to become a woman, if I am going to find happiness."

"Good luck on that. I can't make any suggestions there. What did you do after you left the office?"

"I came back to the shop and continued working."

"You didn't go anywhere else? Who can vouch for you?"

"The owner."

"I'll check with him later," said Clancy folding his notebook up and putting in his jacket. "That will be all for now."

* * * * *

Like a kid at a fire, Greg jumped up all excited from his chair and ran over to Clancy's and David's desks. "I just got a call from Brewery Bay. A little dust up was going on down there. Disturbance of the peace. they need reinforcements. They need our help. Their bouncer can't handle it by himself." Greg rubbed his hands in glee.

Clancy sprang to his feet, getting out his baton and twirling it in the air. "Men, we need some exercise. We need to go in there and swing a little lead with our batons. Bash a few heads together. Show them how the OPP serves and protects the community. Obviously their bouncer can't handle the situation. Greg, are you up for it? You'll develop a big appetite for lunch afterwards. Smack and Stack 'em. That's our motto. Okay men, are you ready?" said Clancy on an adrenaline high.

They rushed down the street to Brewery Bay. "David, you stand guard at the rear exit and pick off any stragglers."

Inside the Brewery Bay bar, the noise was deafening. Over at the bar, two middle aged men with jutting beer bellies were shouting and pushing, bouncing each other back and forth. Clancy recognized one as Eric Badas, the fireman who sanctimoniously claimed to have cut back on his drinking.

"Greg, separate those two. Give it to them good. Don't take any hostages."

Greg dived in amongst the flaying arms of the two men. But his actions were short lived. He screamed in agony as he got a painful kick in the balls which collapsed him into the nearest chair.

"Assaulting a police officer?" asked Clancy then whacked the nearest man hard on his head with his baton. "Are you resisting? If you are, I'll whack you again. Gentlemen, what have we here?" addressing the bar, "Two middle aged men acting like punk kids. Cool off or you'll spend the night in the pokey for breach of the peace."

"This guy," said the one holding his head in his hands looking dazed and confused, pointed at Eric. "He called me a liar and I won't stand for it."

"I did not."

"Yes, you did."

"Gentlemen, it's time to settle down, resolve your differences or leave with handcuffs on. You're disturbing the peace. You decide. Which is it, Eric? Why did you call this man a liar?"

"He said that I was cheating at cards in the fire hall. I wasn't."

"Be what it may. I am surprised to find you in here after you had told me that you had cut back on your drinking."

"I just dropped in for a few minutes. Ask the bar tender. I came to pick up my keys. They had found them on the floor under a chair."

"Yeh, we've heard that one before. That's what they all say. Don't breach your probation and lose your job, Eric. No man is indispensable. I am going to let you off lightly but don't let me see you in here again."

Badas muttered a gruff "Thank you" and left.

His opponent sat in a chair holding his aching head. "I can hardly see. I can feel a big lump on the back of my head. Either I have a concussion or brain damage. I am going to sue for police brutality."

"Who are your witnesses? Point them out to me and I will have a nice little chat with them," said Clancy smacking his baton on his thigh.

"The rest of the bar. Everyone here."

"No one will vouch for their sobriety. Get real. Go home and cool off. As for the rest of you lot, I don't want to come back in here again today to sort things out."

He grabbed Greg who was still in pain and headed out the door. "We showed them, didn't we?"

"Sure did," said Greg clutching his groin. "Sure did. I wonder if I should put ice cubes on it, to stop the swelling. It's very painful."

"Oh, don't act like an old woman. Bear it like a man. It's part of the job."

"Says you." Back at the office, Greg found a whoopee cushion to sit on.

* * * * *

When they had settled in at their desks, Clancy asked about any developments in the break and enter scene.

From his corner at the back of the room Greg hollered, "there has been increased activity in the break and enter area. Some of the homes along the lake have had stuff stolen, like cash sale items, computers, TVs, iPads that sort of thing. It sounds like people wanting an easy sale for drugs."

"Seems like it. How did they get in?"

"The usual. Cottages are not difficult to break into. People are so trusting. They leave their patio doors unsecured. Another point of entry is to smash the basement window. Or smash the small pane of glass in the front door, then reach for the inside lock. Run of the mill. Nothing that requires a great deal of imagination. People are careless. They think that these things don't go on. They don't properly lock up. They leave basement and patio door windows open on hot nights. Picnic tables are left out in the garden for thieves to stand on against a building so the thief can hop on and reach up and open a window. Step ladders are left leaning against the walls. The opportunity is there and the thief takes it. Usually they don't have to smash a pane of glass to get in. It most cases it all boils down to sheer carelessness on the homeowners' part."

"I figure Jimmy Snipe and his pals must be busy. But they won't be lucky all the time and then we'll get them. Let's keep our eyes open. They are like gnats, always flying around, close but not close enough to catch them in the act. They're clever, they wear gloves and they don't leave tracks with their running shoes. For transport, they either use a car or a bicycle. But eventually they slip up and are caught."

Another call came in. Harry Wong, a pharmacist at World Drug Mart was on the line. "Something strange is going on. We have had ten prescriptions for OxyNeo, an opioid which the pharmaceuticals produced when the patent ran out on OxyContin. So far there already have been reports of one death. The prescriptions are signed by the late Dr. Lang. We normally don't fill that many in a week. I thought I should notify you. There's a run on OxyNeo. It looks suspicious."

"That's interesting. Is it his prescription pad? His signature?"

"Yeh, it is his pad but the signature is illegible. It looks like his signature but it's very hard to read a doctor's writing in the first place."

"Put the prescriptions on hold that he has signed. His prescription pad has disappeared since his murder. These are forgeries on a stolen prescription pad."

"I figured that. Thanks for telling me. I will be on the lookout for any more."

"I'll phone some other pharmacies and check with them. Thanks for calling."

Clancy checked with two others and it was the same story a run on NeoContin signed by Dr. Jerry Lang. These were forgeries for sure. He told the pharmacies to stop filling the orders. If a patient needs the drug, they will have to go to another doctor and get a prescription which the doctor probably won't give."

Now to find out who is pushing them? I have a pretty good idea.

* * * * *

Late Saturday afternoon, Clancy felt a bit sleepy at his desk but he snapped to when he heard Greg yelling at him. "Clancy, a 911.call from a guy who calls himself George Smith. Says there's a disturbance at the Mariposa Opera House. He says his son has been sexually assaulted in the men's washroom of the Mariposa Opera House after a Gordon Lightfoot matinee concert."

"I'll be right over. I can't wait to do damage with my baton on some perp."

Parking his car, Clancy pushed through the heavy oak doors on the outside of the turret and tower styled building and then quickly clattered down the stairs to the basement where the washrooms were.

A middle-aged man in sports shirt and slacks and his son were standing outside the men's washroom door, a swing door on hinges. Standing next to him, the son looked to be about 11, a fat pudgy boy with a bad case of acne from eating too many chocolate bars. Seeing Clancy, the father stepped forward. "I'm George Smith and this is my son, Mathew. I called you. My son has just been sexually assaulted in there." He pointed to the door.

"Where is the person who did this? Where did he get to?"

"The pervert didn't get away. Another man has grabbed him and is holding him inside the washroom for us."

"Let me see who it is." Clancy strode into the white tiled washroom.

A heavy set man in a black T shirt and jeans with bulging biceps had wrestled, the youth with his arm pinned up his back against the wall facing the mirror above the urinal. He was struggling to get away but couldn't. "He's breaking my arm." whined the youth.

"You can release him now," said Clancy, "turn around." Clancy recognized him immediately, "Ah, you again. Adam Fair. Not keeping your hands to yourself? Is this your masculine side surfacing? Now, what's the story?" He indicated for the father to begin.

"After the folk concert, my son had to go to the loo. I stood outside and waited for my son to finish. My son was peeing at the urinal and this creep was standing next to him, staring at his dick. He kept moving closer and closer to him. My son turned to leave, to get away. This creep put his hand out to touch his dick. The dirty faggot. My son yelled, keep your hands off me. I rushed in and confronted this creep and got assistance from this another man, Mr. Ford who has been really helpful."

Mr. Ford spoke, "I was happy to oblige. I can't stand men that prey on children."

"I did no such thing. He's lying, making things up. It was the other way round," yelled Adam.

"Sure, it was. Hold your hands behind your back," he said to Adam, and slipped handcuffs on him. "I thought you were going to keep your activities confined to Church Street down in Toronto?"

"I'm being framed."

"Sure you are. A little overnight stay in our jail will cool you off. Then you can try to make bail over in Barrie tomorrow."

"I'm innocent. That 11 year old kid was bothering me. It was the other way around."

"Sure, sure, tell it to the judge tomorrow about attempting to have sex with a minor." Clancy took down the name of the man and his son, the time of the incident and the date and put it in his notebook. He then frog marched Adam out to the patrol car while a few bystanders watched the proceedings. "There's nothing like a captive audience," said Clancy.

At the police station he shut Adam in his cell with two others. "The jail is too crowded to put you in an isolated cell all by yourself. You'll have to go in with the general population. The other inmates like to do nasty things like gang bang to child molesters. To them you are lower than a worm on the ground. If you get released on bail, don't bother to hang around the Opera House washroom again."

Clancy headed back into the office where the phone was ringing. "Just arrested a pervert, Adam Fair, and put him back there behind bars where he belongs. Any sightings on the Trans Canada Trail?"

"Nothing much in the way of witnesses. It is still early days."

Clancy looked into his in-tray. No phone numbers to call. He found his files piled on his desk amongst the paper clips, the stapler, the pens and the scraps of paper. He could smell the garbage pail from where he was sitting. It was full of Tim Horton's paper cups, apple cores and greasy serviettes.

"It needs emptying. This whole office looks like a trash can. Greg, did you hear that? A trash can. It's time to tidy up. I think I will go home and have a nice barbecue, put on the steaks, wrap the corn cobs in silver foil, put on the baked potatoes, the works."

"Are Greg and I invited?" asked David

"Not this time, I want to have a quiet evening."

"Aren't we popular," said David. "We know who our friends are, don't we, Greg?"

"Yeh."

*****

Clancy felt that he was getting nowhere with the interviews that he had with patients so far. I need Nurse Sweet's help. There must have been some altercations in that office between Dr. Lang and his patients. All his sessions couldn't go that smoothly. He must have had some difficult patients. I need to pay Miss Sweet another visit.

An elderly woman on crutches was slowing coming down the steps of the Medical Arts Building so Clancy was able to slip in behind her through the open door without knocking her crutches to the ground, which saved him some time from buzzing the office and then having to wait.

This time he found Dr. Lang's office door wide open. Cartons of files and boxes were stacked up on the carpet. The walls were stripped bare. All the framed diplomas and medical degrees had been taken down from the walls. So much was stacked in boxes it was hard to navigate through to the desk without stepping on a box or a glass frame. His foot squashed down on a manila folder. Miss Sweet was kneeling in a corner, putting white envelopes, into a box. She looked up. "You caught me at a bad time. Brenda Lang asked me to wind up Dr. Lang's affairs by the end of the month when his lease is up. Plus I have to send out the files of patients so that they can hook up with another psychiatrist. I have a lot of work to get done in a short time. I hope this won't take long."

"Did Dr. Lang, do you recall, have, anything usual happen in his office, like a fight or something involving him and his patients that you were witness to?"

"Why yes now that you mentioned it. about a month ago, Mr. Small came in. Dr. Lang felt that he was becoming addicted to his medication and wanted to slowly cut back on it. Not abruptly, because that induces psychosis in the case of Prozac which can be quite dangerous if a patient is rapidly cut off. They have scientific evidence to prove it. Some patients become suicidal if they are immediately cut off. Dr. Lang was just going to adjust the dose downward.

"Mr. Small was none too happy about this change of events. I need my medication. I am lost without it, he said. Dr.

Lang patiently explained the addictive properties of this particular drug and that starting that day he would try to wean Mr. Small from it. It is for your own good, for your own mental health, he told him.

"But Small couldn't seem to grasp what he was telling him. Instead he became very agitated He grabbed the paper knife on Dr. Lang's desk and stabbed himself in the wrist. Dr. Lang pressed the emergency buzzer and I rushed in. Warm blood was soon everywhere, on the carpet, on the chair and on the wall. We got Mr. Small to calm down and sent him to emergency at Soldiers Memorial. It was a real emergency. Mr. Small recovered and has a small scar on his wrist now but it was a very high adrenalin based incident. There was all that blood in the office to clean up. He never threatened Dr. Lang with the penknife."

"What will he do now?"

"Find another psychiatrist. He can't blame Dr. Lang for his suicidal outburst. There were many things in his life that precipitated this depression, not just one thing that triggered it. One can't point a finger and say that caused it."

"I see. Can you recall any other episode in the office that happened in the last six months?

"Yes, there were others. I am trying to think. There was an altercation with Mrs. Holly Jones."

"Tell me about it "

"Well Mrs. Jones had the idea that she was in love with Dr. Lang. This is quite common. Many women patients fall in love with their doctor. But her delusion or fantasy was that he reciprocated her feelings. She asked for private time with him to explore both their feelings. In other words she propositioned him.

He explained very patiently to her, that he was only a mirror to herself. She did not know him except in a clinical setting, meeting once a week in his office for fifty minutes. The rest was all fantasy. Part of successful therapy is positive transference, transferring the patient's feelings onto the therapist, to become enamoured with the therapist. It happens a lot especially between a woman and her doctor. He explained that he was here to help her, to help her overcome her addiction. But she was stubborn, She didn't want to take no for an answer. He didn't tell her that he would lose his medical license if he got involved with her sexually. Dr. Lang had to proceed very slowly and carefully with this woman. He alerted me to the fact that there might be trouble and that he was having difficulty. She was a very sexual provocative woman, not used to being denied what she wanted. She was a femme fatale. Underneath it all she was as hard as nails."

"Did anything happen?"

"No, the therapy continued but she often left the office in a huff. She was very short with me and snappish. She had the same appointment time every two weeks. I wrote out the little card each time and gave it to her. She whipped it out of my hand. She was frustrated in not getting her own way. She was a frustrated and angry woman is how I would put it."

"Do you think that she held a grudge against Dr. Lang?"

"Well she wasn't too happy with the way things were not going to her liking."

"Do you think she could commit a violent act, like murder?"

"It's hard to say."

"Did you come across his prescription pad among his things? Can I see it?"

"It usually is kept in the top drawer." She reached the desk and opened the drawer. That's strange. It's not in there. I don't recall taking it out of there."

"When was the last time you saw it?"

"That Friday afternoon. I will check Dr. Lang's appointment book for that day he died. Here is a list of all the patients. That might help me to recall that afternoon."

"Does this include everyone that came into the office that afternoon?"

"I have to think? Mm, I recall a youth coming in between patients, just briefly, Jimmy Snipes. Yes, he came in between patients to pick up a prescription," he said. That's why his name is not in the book."

"Do you recall his visit at all?"

"Very briefly. He came in and went."

"Do you know what it was about?"

"No."

"And that was the last time you saw the prescription pad that you recall?"

"Yes."

"Mm," thought Clancy. "Dollars to doughnuts, Jimmy Snipes has stolen the prescription pad."

"Was Dr. Lang upset at all that last afternoon? Anything unusual? Anything happen that was different? You were the last person to see him alive."

"No, he was the same as usual. He was a very kind man to work for. Oh, if I only could have done something to prevent it." She wiped a tear away from her eye.

"You had feelings for him."

"Yes, I loved him. But he was a married man and that was that. Maybe if he wasn't married things could have been different."

"I understand. Do you think he felt the same way?"

"It was never put on the table for discussion."

"One last question. Has your office ever been broken into by people looking for drugs?"

"Yes, we had one break in at the beginning of the year. They were looking for drugs and we don't keep a large supply on the premises."

"Did you ever have coffee with Dr. Lang outside this office?"

She nodded her head. "Maybe once in a blue moon."

"Do you think anybody spotted you talking to Dr. Lang? No matter how innocent, word could have gotten back to his wife. It's a small town."

"We were very discreet. We were very careful. We didn't arrive together nor did we leave together."

"She may have found out. Did you and Mrs. Lang ever meet?"

"Not exactly."

"Explain."

"She phoned me a week before he died – wanted to talk to me. She said it was urgent, but I didn't want to talk to her."

"Did she tell you what it was about?"

"No, just said it was urgent and did not want to discuss

it on the phone. I put her off."

"So you never did meet?"

"No, then Dr. Lang was murdered."

"I see."

Clancy sensed something was not quite right. But what? She had lied about something and he couldn't put his finger on what.

*****

After talking to Miss Sweet, Clancy decided that they should have another look at Mr. Small. The other side of the coin from depression was anger.

"David," said Clancy, "I want you to go over and have another chat with Mr. Small. See what he has to say about the penknife incident in Dr. Lang's office. There might be something more to it."

David retraced his steps up the walk to Mr. Small's house to have another chat, just in case he had overlooked something. Mr. Small had had an explosive encounter with Dr. Lang. David knocked and waited. When Mr. Small came to the door, David found him in the same state as he had found him before. He smelled of sweat and hadn't shaved. He was wearing the same dirty clothes, trousers with suspenders and a greyish undershirt. This man should get a grip on himself, he thought.

"You again. I told you all I know."

"I want to ask just a few more questions to help us in our inquiries."

He followed Small back to the kitchen and sat down.

"I heard that you stabbed yourself with a paper knife in Dr. Lang's office. Were you trying to commit suicide? Or what?"

"Yeh, I am ashamed to say I was desperate. I was being cut off my drug supply."

"Not exactly and that's not the way I heard it. That's your version."

Mr. Small held his sweaty face in his hands. "I guess that I overreacted."

"Let me see your arms. Roll up your sleeves."

Mr. Small reluctantly did so and held out his arms.

"There are a few cuts here. Did you do that?"

"Yes, I can't stop myself sometimes."

"You've got to pull yourself together and find another therapist."

"Waiting lists are endless."

"Go to emergency and ask for one. Where are your kitchen knives kept?"

"On that magnetic strip over there on the side wall above the counter."

David walked over to examine them." How many do you have?"

"Five."

He could see that none was missing in the rack.

"Someone stabbed Dr. Lang with a kitchen knife."

"Well it's not me. Mine are all there."

"Mr. Small, you need professional help and you must get it soon. Go to Barrie General's outpatient clinic and see if you can't get a psychiatrist that way, one whose list is open and taking patients."

"I hadn't thought of that."

"Go, before you do something foolish." David let himself out.

* * * * *

It was a slow afternoon so Clancy announced to the office," it's time we staked out the Too Tired Pool Hall. I am getting a report that there are may be active drug pushers in there. Some have a whole pharmacy up their sleeve pushing OxyNeo and cocaine. We can't have that. I'm itching to use my baton on those layabouts."

"Me too," said Greg. "Bring it on."

"Now here's the plan."

They walked up the laneway leading to the pool hall and swung the door open. "Get a couple of officers on the fire exit. Two of us will go in the front door to see what they're selling over the counter. Normally they would lose their license for selling illegal drugs but on the other hand it is very convenient for us that the pool hall stays open. We don't have to go looking too far."

They stood against the door whacking their batons on their thighs, taking everyone in around the room. "Whack them and stack them." But there were only two players at the pool table, the rest were sitting at small tables, nursing beers looking as meek as mice. "We're not looking for any trouble," said the manager rushing over. "How can I help you? What's the problem?"

"We believe drug pushers looking for clients are in here," replied Clancy. "Aha, look who is here." Clancy strode over to the pool table and clamped his hand on one of the player's shoulders who had his back to him. "Isn't this a coincidence? Just passing the time of day, Jimmy? A little pool must be bad for the back when you bend over, eh? It must be painful. Take off your jacket. Don't be shy. You've got nothing to hide. Easy does it. Check all the pockets." He handed the jacket over to David.

"Spread your legs. Up against the wall. Get a free goosing. Ah. Ha. Some OxyNeo tablets just fell out of your trouser pocket, Jimmy. For personal use? Eh? Dr. Lang's prescription pad has disappeared. I wonder where it went to. It disappeared the same day he was murdered."

"I had nothing to do with his murder. I already told you I was in his office for just fifteen minutes."

"Me and you, Jimmy are going to sit down and have a nice little chat at the police station."

"I have my rights. You can't pin this murder on me. I am being set up."

"Oh, Jimmy, justice will prevail. Everyone is innocent until proven guilty. No one is guilty unless proven otherwise. You have been reading too many newspaper articles about too many murder trials where the innocent guy goes straight to the electric chair. Jimmy, you come along nicely with me and tell me how you laid your hot little hands on Dr. Lang's prescription pad that was in his desk. Did you do it when his back was turned? You must have moved fast. How quick you are and how light fingered as well."

He called out to the others. "Have we found any more drugs?"

"Not so far. Clean."

"Well I have got one and we are going to have a nice little chat. Let's go, Jimmy. It will all depend on how cooperative you will be."

*****

Clancy led Jimmy into the office and pointed to a chair in front of his desk for him to sit down on. "Make yourself comfortable, Jimmy. It might be a long chat."

Greg looked up from his desk. "Hey Clancy, Bob White came over, checking on developments. He wants to be kept informed. He needs a written report by tomorrow. "

"He does, does he? I am not providing Bob White with reading material. I have a million things to do." He turned to Jimmy. "Now where was I? Well Jimmy, my lad, Dr. Lang's prescription pad has disappeared and all over Mariposa, at drugstores, prescriptions for OxyNeo are showing up with Dr. Lang's forged signature on the bottom of them. The prescription pad with his signature on the bottom is worth a lot of money to somebody. Lo and behold after the prescription pad disappeared, a couple of hours later, Dr. Lang was murdered."

"Well I had nothing to do with it."

"But you did take his subscription pad."

"Who says so? Have you got any witnesses?"

"I say so. You're the last person to get a prescription. Then the pad disappears."

"You can't pin that on me."

"We can pin possession and trafficking in narcotics on you."

"I have a prescription."

"Yeh, make sure it is for the prescribed amount. We'll keep digging, Jimmy. Something is bound to stick to the wall." Clancy smacked his hand hard on the desk.

"Yeh, like police harassment."

"Keep, your nose clean, Jimmy. I can't charge you for the NeoContin because you have got a prescription for it but that doesn't stop me from looking for the prescription pad and when I find it, you are toast."

"Not in this lifetime. I haven't got it and I have already been searched. I have my rights."

Clancy opened the door and let that skinny little weasel out onto the street. "We'll be in touch, Jimmy, Don't go too far. This is not the first and last little chat we will have. Your kind I always see again. It's like revolving doors."

* * * * *

A teen aged girl with a pony tail bounced through the door, holding out a large dirty black leather bag which she laid on the counter.

"Is this the Lost and Found?" she asked in a shrill voice.

"Yes, miss, you've come to the right place. What have you got for us?" asked Clancy getting a peek down her low-cut peasant drawstring blouse when she bent over to show him, a sight he found most pleasing. If he kept this up, he'd go blind and be labeled a dirty old man.

"I found this bag in a ditch out by Concession 1 where it intersects with the Trans Canada Trail."

"Why is a pretty girl like you wandering in a ditch?"

"You must be joking. My mother was driving me down there for me to jog and I happened to look out the window and saw it. Mother stopped the car and I went and retrieved it."

"Well, thanks for bringing it in. If there is a reward, I will let you know. Leave me your name and phone number."

The girl wrote down her name and phone number on a piece of paper and handed it to him. Then she waved goodbye, "Mother's waiting for me."

Clancy examined the purse. It had large handles on the outside. Hard to say what age the owner might be. He drew back the zipper and opened the purse.

A wallet. Ah it is unusual to find a wallet. Usually this is thrown away. Inside were the cards. A social insurance number for Miss Temple, an OHIP card, several credit cards and five dollars folded in another sleeve of the purse. Strange, nothing seems to be missing.

So this was Miss Temple's purse. It was probably dropped when she was attacked. This is where Jerry Lang's car was and where we think he was killed. It doesn't look like robbery.

At the moment as a witness, she is useless. She's got amnesia and can't remember a thing. But she will be glad to get her purse back, the poor old dear. She reminds me of my mother on her good days.

Clancy walked over to David's desk and handed over the purse. "It belongs to Miss Temple. Would you return it to her, please and see if she remembers anything more?"

"So far, she hasn't remembered a thing."

"Well, it has been several weeks now, so maybe, just maybe she might."

David got up from his desk. "Yes, I will go over to the hospital and see if she is still there."

David drove over, took the elevator up to her floor to be greeted by that cute nurse Shelly with the blue eyes and freckles. If he wasn't already involved, he'd definitely be interested. With a big smile, she said, "Hi there, it is good to see you again."

"Me, too. I have come to see Miss Temple and ask her a few questions."

"You're just in time. This afternoon she is going to be discharged." She walked with him into the room. "Miss Temple, I have got someone to see you, a visitor."

"Hi, I'm Dave Scott of the OPP. I have brought you, your purse that was stolen. Can you check to see if anything is missing? They found it in a ditch on Concession Road, near the Trans Canada Trail. Would you like me to get you a cold glass of water?"

"No, that won't be necessary." Miss Temple sat upright. "My purse, my purse." She grabbed at it and opened it. "I don't keep much money in my purse, not that I have any. So far so good. Nothing seems to have been taken. My OHIP card is here and my birth certificate, a package of Kleenex and my comb. A couple of safety pins. I always keep some in case of an emergency. I also keep $5.00 hidden amongst my cards and it is here." She held up the bill. "Now I am anxious to get home. The things in my refrigerator are all spoiled and who knows if someone broke into my place while I have lain here."

"I don't think so. We had a patrol car drive by your house every so often, just checking that the house was secure."

"What about my pussy, Gloria? Is it still alive?"

"I understand a kind neighbor is feeding it."

"I have wanted to go home long ago, but they have kept me in here."

"It's up to the doctors," said Nurse Shelley. "They make the decisions. They know when you are ready."

David spoke, "I have some questions for you Miss Temple. I hope they can stir your memory. Can I take you back to that afternoon when you went for a walk? Was the day cloudy or sunny? Where did you go for a walk?"

Miss Temple shook her head.

"Do you remember walking along the trail, anything that you noticed on the trail? Anything that caught your attention or that you stopped and looked at?"

Miss Temple shook her head again.

"Do you recall talking to anyone on the trail? Did anyone pass you on the trail? A man? A woman? Or some youths? Did anyone approach you? Do you recall talking to anyone?"

"It is all a blank. I remember nothing at all. I can't even remember going for a walk."

"This happens to patients who have received blows to the head," said Nurse Shelly. "She may never remember what has happened."

"I see," said David. "The main thing is you are well enough to go home. That's the good news. I must be on my way, Ms. Shelly, it has been a pleasure meeting you and thanks for your time, Miss Temple. I hope that you are up and about, soon." David walked down the hall and got into the elevator. He sighed and thought, we're no further ahead in this investigation.

* * * * *

Greg polished off his Macintosh apple then threw the core into the waste basket, just missing it. He got up to retrieve it off the floor but then the phone rang. He'd pick the apple core up later. He reached for the phone "Miss Sweet on the line for you, Clancy. Is she as sweet as her name implies? She says she has got more info for you?" He put his hand over the mouthpiece. He leered at Clancy. "Is that all she is phoning about?"

Clancy shook his head, mouthed the word busy. "Will you take it this time, David? I got to run down a few errands first."

"Constable David Scott here. Detective Clancy Murphy is otherwise engaged."

"Hello. I forgot to mention to Detective Clancy one patient that threatened Dr. Lang shortly after she came to be his patient. It was her first appointment. She said that she would kill herself and him. She had a knife with her."

"That's interesting. Tell me more."

"Yes. She carried it in her backpack."

"What kind of knife was it?"

"A regular kitchen knife."

"Yes, that sounds promising," said David. "How did he handle the situation?"

"Dr. Lang turned on the intercom so that I could hear the conversation without her knowing. He told her that there was no need for that. He wanted to be her friend and to help her. She calmed down after a while and put it away."

"Did she ever bring it into the office again?"

"Not that I was aware of. Nor did Dr. Lang mention it."

"She has a troubled background. A 17 year old high school dropout, Debbie is into self-mutilation. She was sexually abused by her stepfather and her uncle as a child. Worked sometimes as a prostitute until she was arrested and then the judge put her on probation."

"She might have the potential for violence. Where can I find her?"

"She can be located at the Adult Learning Centre during the day or the Women's shelter at night. I think she might make a good suspect."

"Thanks, Miss Sweet, I will contact her. It might be worthwhile to drive over there and interview her, to see if she continued to hold a grudge against Dr. Lang."

"Here's the address. It is in an industrial complex on the outskirts of town."

David drove over and found the building, a low lying brick structure, a former school now an adult learning academy for drop outs wanting to pick up high school credits and earn their diplomas. Inside the building the walls despite needing fresh paint, were decorated with cheerful bright coloured posters. Down the hall, a bronze sign said, "Principal's office." He opened the door and greeted the female receptionist. Flashing his ID he said, I'm looking for a young woman named Debbie Young that I want to interview."

"I'll check her timetable. One moment please." She scrolled down through the students names on her computer. "She's in class now but I could ask her to come to the office. There is a small room next to this one that you could use for your interview. It has a table and chairs."

"Great."

He didn't have to wait long before Debbie slouched into the room a teenage rebel without a cause. One side of Debbie's head had been shaved, on the other side, her long black hair was held back with a silver clip. A silver nose ring was attached to her lip and one large tattoo, a black dragon, covered her forearm

"You wanna speak to me?" Her eyes were angry and her tone belligerent. David indicated a seat. She sat down and picked at a scab on her bare arm. He noticed the bitten fingernails on her hands. "I am attending classes and keeping out of trouble. Why are you bothering me?"

"My name is Constable David Scott." He flashed his ID "I am trying to put together a picture of Dr. Lang who was murdered."

"Yeh, I heard. Why him? Why ask me? "

"You were a patient of Dr. Lang's. Can you tell me about the last time you saw him?"

"Last Thursday."

"Why did you go to see him?" David quietly sat and waited for her to say something.

"Do you really want to know or are you just asking that

question to be polite?"

David didn't answer.

Debbie scratched at her arm some more.

"Do you feel that he was helping you?" asked David.

"Yes. He was helping me feel good about myself. He was helping my self-image, so I wouldn't hurt or cut myself."

"When was the last time you were there?"

"Last Thursday after school. I got out of school early and took the bus to his office."

"Did you notice anything different in his manner or appearance? Did you notice anything out of the ordinary or unusual?"

"No, I entered his private office. He indicated a chair that I was to sit down on, and then he asked how my week had been going. I began telling him as I usually do." She chewed on her knuckle and played with the leather bracelet on her wrist. "I sensed, he seemed unhappy, rather depressed, just going through the motions, it's hard to pick up on what he is feeling. He is trained not to reveal his feelings, but one gets the odd impression. Coming from the same territory I can pick up on these things."

"So there was nothing out of the ordinary?"

"No, except I thought that he was a little sad. Nothing that I can put my finger on."

"Did you like him?"

"Yes, he was a kind man."

"How did you get an appointment with him in the first place?"

"I was referred to him after my last arrest by Children's Aid. It was one of the conditions I had to make for a reduced sentence. I was placed on probation. I didn't want to go at first but I am glad I did."

"Do you know of any enemies that Dr. Lang might have had?"

"No, he didn't seem to be the kind of man that would have any enemies."

"Debbie, at your first interview with Dr. Lang, you brought a knife with you and threatened to kill him and yourself. What was that all about?"

"I thought you would get around to that. It is in his notes. I have explained it a thousand times to the police and everyone else. I wasn't going to kill him. I wasn't going to hurt him. I just did it to threaten him. He didn't press charges."

"But you brought the knife with you and you took it out. That could have been grounds for charges to be laid against you and you could have lost your probation and chance to go back to school."

"I wasn't thinking properly. I was in a daze, I was out of control. But Dr. Lang was very nice to me. He didn't press charges. I was desperately unhappy. I feel much calmer now. I was on drugs and just lost my cool. I was coming off them."

"So from that day you never took a knife to the office or carried one? What did you do with the knife?"

"I threw it away in a field where no one could find it."

"Can you take me to the place where you threw it?"

"That was over two years ago and I can't remember the exact place. It was on the Trans Canada Trail, down by the lake. I just jogged by and dropped it in amongst the bushes and grasses."

"So you have not been in the possession of a knife since?"

"No, it was just that one time. I have used razor blades to cut my arms but never a knife."

"We'll keep in touch, Debbie. "I may want to ask more questions. If you can think of anything, let me know. Here's my card,"

Debbie took it and put it into her jean's pocket. 'I hope you catch the person who did this. Dr. Lang was a kind man and didn't deserve this fate. But there is nothing more to tell you. I have told you everything."

"Thanks, Debbie."

She pocketed the card in her jeans jacket. "Am I free to go now back to class?"

David nodded. Nothing here much to go on. Unless there's more to this story than meets the eye. There's no motive. He was helping her.

* * * * *

Clancy was sitting at his desk thinking, I want my lighter back and I know who has got it. It was time to interview Mrs. Holly Jones again and to retrieve it. He had to be careful how he handled her. She was a hottie and had trouble written all over her face.

He drove up the circular driveway. Parked his car and stood at the door, and lifted the knocker several times. He heard her stiletto heels approaching on the parquet hall floor. Then the door flung open. Making a dramatic entrance, Mrs. Jones her breasts peeking through her low cut white nylon blouse and tight black Capri trousers stood there framing the door in a cloud of Channel No. 5.

"I've come to ask you a few more questions, Mrs. Jones. Among other things, I've come to retrieve is my sterling silver lighter. It was given to me by my father for a high school graduation present. He is dead now and I want it back for sentimental reasons." He gave her a tight smile as he held out his hand.

She put her hands on her hips. "Do you think I have it?" She looked him up and down challenging him.

"Most certainly I do. I loaned it to you the last time I was here."

"Oh, well, if you insist. Let me check in my purse." She went to the hall table where her big black leather purse was and began rummaging around in the depths of it, sifting through wallets, coin purse, make up kit, Kleenex, "Ah, found it." She held up the lighter. "I wondered who that belonged to. Sorry." And she handed it over to him.

Clancy quickly pocketed the lighter. "I have several more questions to ask. You mentioned that you did not see anybody in the late afternoon of the 13th.

"Yes, that is correct. I have no alibi."

Do you have your own car?"

"Yes, my husband has his car and I have mine."

"Where can I find your husband?"

"He's in a group real estate practice in Barrie. He is a real estate lawyer."

"May I have his phone number and where I can find him?"

She let her tongue slowly travel along her lower lip. "He works long hours, dealing in the sale of homes and commercial real estate properties. The best time is here later in the evening when he is home. I will look for his business card in the top drawer of his desk in the den and give it to you." She jumped up and went into the next room to fetch it.

"Here it is." She sat down flicking one leg over the other. "He works long hours," she raised an eyebrow, "and he might be hard to get hold of."

"Where was he on the afternoon of June 19th?"

"You will have to ask him. I can't keep up with his comings and goings. It will be hard to catch him. He's in and out."

"Thanks."

"I have a lot of free time. Drop in anytime. I'll be glad to help you with your investigations." She gave him a heavy lidded stare. "I'm home alone a lot and my husband gets home tired and worn out. He's a spent penny when he gets here, if you get my meaning." She crossed and uncrossed her long, slim legs.

Clancy got the message.

"You've been most co-operative, Mrs. Jones. Keep in touch." He headed for the door thankful to make his escape. Back at the office, Clancy put in a call to Barrie. "I wish to speak to Mr. Hugh Jones."

The female receptionist answered. "I'm afraid he won't be in until three o'clock. He is out with a client. Can I ask who is calling?"

"Just tell him that I will call back at 3."

Shortly after 3 pm, Clancy called back." I'll put you through now." said the receptionist.

"Mr. Jones, I am investigating the murder of Dr. Jerry Lang."

"Yes, I heard about it."

"Your wife is a patient of Dr. Lang's."

"Yes, she is."

"Do you feel she was benefiting from the therapy?"

"Yes, Dr. Lang had most impressive credentials."

"May I ask you where you were on the afternoon of June 19th?"

"Let me look at my day book. It will take a few minutes. Here I found it. I was seeing a client who wanted to buy a house. I was drawing up documents for him to sign."

"Can you give me his name and how I can contact him?"

"Yes, I don't think there would be a problem. Dr. Hugh Garner, here in Barrie. Am I a suspect?"

"Everyone is a suspect in a murder case. It's for purposes of elimination."

"I see."

The next call was to Dr. Hugh Garner's office. Clancy explained the purpose of his call to the receptionist, the whereabouts of Dr. Garner, on the afternoon of June 19th.

"He had an appointment with Mr. Hugh Jones about the sale of his house, between the hours of 3.30 and 4.30, the rest of the time he was busy with patients."

So that alibi for Hugh Jones holds up. But Mrs. Jones has no alibi. Keep digging.

* * * * *

It was a full moon that shone in the night sky. A slight breeze blew up from the lake. Black crows were cawing, an owl hooted in the background, crickets were jumping in the long grasses and one could hear the distinct cry of the loon echoing across the water. Then a dark cloud passed over the moon, blotting it out and then the night was suddenly in darkness, so dark that only the taillights of the boats in the harbour could be seen. Visibility was zero. It was not a good night for visiting the marina. Evil walked in the dark.

The next morning the sky was a clear blue. It was David's day off. He looked out the window at the sun shining down. It was the beginning of a beautiful day. It was warm but not too humid. So far there had been no black flies and just the odd mosquito had shown up in June. .It had not been a wet June, which was needed for breeding. The black flies would arrive in August usually in cottage country.

It was a good day for fishing. David parked his car in the municipal parking lot by the marina, which thankfully had no parking meters to fill, got out his fishing tackle from the trunk .slapped some sun tan oil on his face and put on his sun hat. His father had had chunks of skin and flesh excised by the surgeon for melanoma on his nose and forehead. The trouble with melanoma is there is always the fear that the surgeon didn't get it all and that it is still lurking somewhere hidden in the body ready to pop up again, more deadly than the last time.

    David headed down to the Mariposa dock and marina which was filled with boats that had come across from Michigan and other American resort areas along the lake early Friday night.

    Getting down on his hands and knees he peered into the dark water to see if there were any fish, such as minnows, swimming underneath the dock, which was always a good sign of the presence of larger fish. He thought he would try his hand at catching some trout. He walked along the wooden dock a bit further towards the end for he had seen a large dark shadow in the water by one of the posts. He wasn't sure what it was. It could be a big fish. But it was probably a black garbage bag dumped from the boats. He went back to shore and got a long pole to be used as a stick to prod this heavy object and bring it slowly up to the surface. He pushed hard underneath the object until part of it hit the surface with a splash. It wasn't a big fish. He looked again. A dead man's face stared back at him. It gave him somewhat of a shock. Attached to the head was a body floating in the water which had been trapped by one of the underwater pillars.

    He phoned Clancy. "We'll have to pull out the body. Need help in getting it out. It's a young man. I can't do it by myself."

    "How long has it been in the water?"

    "It's hard to say. Maybe just over night. There are quite a few boats moored nearby and the body couldn't have been here long or it would have been spotted earlier. People who are murdered are usually dumped in plastic bags weighed down by rocks to hide the body so it won't be discovered for a while. This one wasn't."

    "Is the water very deep there?"

    "It is deep enough. I don't think we will need a diver.

It's in plain sight, and not down resting on the bottom of the lake. Just get a fire crew here with a long hook and then have them drag the body out of the water. We can lay him out on the dock and then turn him over to the coroner and let him take it from there."

In a short time, the firemen arrived in a truck and used a long hook to snag the floater under his arms, pull him away from the post and then drag the body near the dock where they could lift him up and lie him down on the boards.

A wave of green algae and slimy debris came up with the sagging body which smelled to high heaven. Green water rushed out of its clothing, dripping puddles around David's feet. The sight was nauseating. David gagged at the sight and smell.

When they laid the body onto a black plastic body bag, Clancy had a good look at his face before zipping it shut. "I know this guy. It's our friend the town pervert, Adam Fair. Well, well, he has joined the world of the fishes. I wonder how it all happened. Did he fall in or was he pushed? We'll have to wait for the coroner to make that decision."

* * * * *

"Canada Day, July 1st weekend is coming up soon with lots of fireworks down at the park. Are you going to put up the Maple Leaf flag and sing O Canada, Clancy? Are you going to have a barbecue in the back yard, eat tons of watermelon and get loaded? Are you going to take some time off?"

"Not with a murder case still unsolved, Greg."

Then the phone rang. "Dr. Frost, the coroner, on the line for you, Clancy," said Greg. "Have a good day,"

"Until now."

"Now where has my report gone?" said Dr. Frost, pushing papers around." Bear with me, will you, Clancy. I had it right here on my desk. Ah! I found it among all the files piled up here. I gather you knew the floater. There is no ID on him."

"He was known to police. The name is Adam Fair. He was up recently on a sexual molestation charge, an incident at the Mariposa Opera House."

"Ah yes, fondling a young boy, as I recall. Nasty. The floater had a slight concussion on the back of his head. He could have gotten it when he fell in hitting his head against the dock. He has a high blood alcohol count and there is water in his lungs. He was alive when he went in. There are two scenarios for you. He tripped and fell into the water and drowned or someone hit him on the back of the head and pushed him in. He might not have been able to swim. There are no injuries on his body anywhere else, except that bump which he might have gotten from hitting something in the water."

"Do you think he was pushed off the dock or fell?"

"It's hard to say. He had a high blood alcohol count and he may have just tripped on a board or nail and fallen in. Not being able to swim, he drowned."

"How long has he been in the water?"

"Not long, otherwise the decomposing body buoyed up by body gases would have floated to the surface. He has been in the water twenty four hours maximum. There is very little decomposition. No fishes have attacked his eyes."

"Ugh," said Clancy. "Well sum it up."

"I have written here in my report an open verdict. *Death by misadventure.*"

"Thanks. I will try to find some witnesses for Friday evening. There are a lot of boats moored by, maybe somebody saw something. I'll ask around."

Clancy got up from his desk and put his jacket on. Time for a little spin down to the marina and see what he could come up with.

He began his investigation by knocking on the boat hulls and cabins of various boats, moored near the dock in the yacht basin. There were at least ten rows of boats to cover. "Hello, hello, anybody home?" No response. Obviously they were empty, their owners had gone ashore to get groceries or shopping at the nearby liquor store conveniently located just steps from the harbour. Then he heard someone yell, "You're trespassing on my property. What do you want?" A grey haired man peered out at him from behind canvas.

"I'm from the OPP. Did you hear any noise last night?

Were men arguing or fighting?"

"Nope. I'm from Michigan, just having a cocktail with my old lady. How can I help you?"

"There's been an accident off the dock, Someone fell in."

"It was really quiet last evening, lots of seagulls diving and flapping around overhead, only sound was lapping of water against the hull of the boat and the sound of the odd motorboat in the distance."

"Did you hear two men arguing?"

"The only noise I heard was a big splash around 11 pm which I thought was a fish and didn't bother to investigate. Has this got anything to do with the guy who drowned?"

"Yes, that's why I am here. Thanks anyway. I will keep trying to find somebody who may have heard something."

He came to the last boat to call at. Maybe I will get lucky. Clancy went and knocked on the cabin door. An old geezer wearing a sailor's cap stuck his head out. "What can I do for you, son?"

"Did you hear anything suspicious last night? Men arguing, shouting or fighting?"

"This is pretty peaceful around here. That's why I come. Nothing like that around here. There is just the sound of sea gulls, an owl or a loon. I didn't hear a thing."

Clancy thanked him. It looks like there were no witnesses.

With no witnesses there can be no search. Unless something interesting bubbles to the surface, or a witness comes forward, I am going to leave it at that. Who knows what Adam Fair's state of mind was? There are other more important things that I have to attend to.

* * * * *

Clancy's mind was still on his dog, Mike. When he came to let him out this morning for a run, Mike didn't get up. Those big brown eyes stayed closed. Mike had breathed his last. Where should he bury his beloved dog? Probably the best place would be in the back yard underneath the cherry tree.

He would do it this evening when he got home from work. Wrap Mike up in his favourite blanket, toss in a bone, then get a shovel and put him in the ground. Later he would think of some marker that he would place there.

Looking out the window, he could see the heavy rain pelting down, good for the plants. But with the rain came increased humidity which made it muggy in the office despite the air conditioning. Greg had forgotten his umbrella and damned if he was going to go out in this weather to buy the coffee and doughnuts. Let some other sucker go.

The phone rang. He let Greg pick up the phone. "A call has come in. Traffic accident at Mississauga and Peter." Clancy called out, "David. You take it. I was suppose to write a report for Bob White and haven't got around to it. Keep putting it off, running out of excuses, such a waste of my time, so many things to do, so little time. On top of which I have to kiss ass with him when he comes over when I really want to kick him in the ass."

"You've got to get organized."

"Yeh, you're a great one to talk. Look at your desk. It's an absolute mess."

"What's this accident about?"

"A pedestrian has been injured."

David drove over to the intersection, taking just a few minutes to get there. The ambulance was on the scene before him. Two ambulance crew were loading the victim onto a stretcher, doing CPR at the same time. An oxygen mask was covering the injured man's mouth. David walked over to the ambulance and asked to see the guy's wallet, probably in his jacket. Someone mentioned that the old guy had been wearing earphones crossing the street.

How many times had they warned the public about wearing ear phones listening to music crossing a busy intersection? His photo ID said Mr. Edwin Small of Brant Street. I interviewed him. It's Dr. Lang's patient, the depressive. I should have recognized him. But the oxygen mask covered his face."

"Is he badly injured?"

"We put an IV on him but his internal organs would feel

the impact of the collision. There is no telling how serious the internal bleeding will be. Or for that matter his head injuries. Only an X-ray will tell us the whole story. Look at his eyes fluttering open and shut. He is drifting in and out of consciousness."

David closed the doors and the ambulance sped off.

David looked for signs of a collision. A large delivery truck for LCBO had stopped at point of impact showing a few black skid marks on the pavement surrounded by broken glass strewn across the asphalt. Its right front fender was bent.

The truck driver, a man in his early thirties in jeans and jacket, was sitting on the curb holding his head in shock and disbelief. "I tried to stop. I thought he could see me."

"Go over slowly what happened."

"I was going real slow in turning the corner into the right bound lane. The old guy had his head phones on listening to music. He didn't see my truck I slowed down and he kept on going, right into me. He didn't stop. This is terrible. I just feel awful."

"I have to give you a breath analyzer test. Drunk any alcohol today? No? Well this will tell us. Here breathe into this." He waited. "The results are negative. If all is what you say it is, there may be no charges. We have warned the public about the dangers of wearing head phones on the street and in traffic so many times. "

He looked around at the gathered crowd. "Did anyone see this happen?"

A woman on the edge of the crowd with a push buggy full of groceries said that she was standing on the corner behind the victim and saw him step off the curb without looking. "He didn't pay attention to the lights when they had changed."

Another person yelled out, "The old guy didn't look where he was going. "

"Well it looks like it is Small's fault. I will write up my report and list the collision as an accident. Later I will contact the hospital and see how he is doing."

The hospital emergency nurse said that they were X-raying him, but he had a lot of internal injuries, liked crushed ribs, ruptured spleen, broken leg and arm. He was a high risk if they operated. Things did not look good.

David updated Clancy on Small's condition. "It may be better this way for Small to die than to live. For him living is too painful."

"Whatever. He will be in the hospital a long time recuperating. That takes care of one suspect. We know where he will be for the next little while."

* * * * *

Clancy was deep in thought. "Greg, today I have come to a big decision."

"New developments in the Lang murder case?"

"No, you idiot. I mean about buying a dog. I miss having a dog so much. I miss the affection. I was always a dog man. I miss Mike but he is dead and buried in the back yard. It is time to move on."

"I hope you don't go out and buy a poodle, or a Pekinese. That kind of dog wouldn't go well with your image."

"No, those kind of dogs I have never liked. They are too feminine and too hairy fairy. I can't stand their nervous yapping. I want a dog that is a man dog, good for security and is affectionate."

"There should be plenty of those around. Have you thought of the pound? Most dogs before you adopt them have been given their shots which might save you a bit of money. Or you can spend the bucks and get a pure bred, not a mongrel."

"Mike was a mongrel and a wonderful dog."

"I am not suggesting anything."

"Going to the pound is not a bad idea. I am going to take a break and go over to the animal rescue centre and see what they've got."

* * * * *

Clancy found the animal shelter on Mississauga. He could hear the howl of the dogs as he approached the door. A sign on the door said, *'You need a pet. A pet needs you.'* Some wit had crossed out the, 'a' and changed it to 'to'.

A red, green, yellow feathered parrot was chained to the top of a pole. The parrot was squawking, "Fuck off, fuck off." Below its perch was a sign, Not for Sale.

A hamster in its cage was whirling around on a mini circus wheel uncertain as how to get off.

In a nest of wood shavings, a group of tiny guinea pigs were doing what guinea pigs do. They mate more frequently than rabbits thought Clancy.

A rabbit cage with baby rabbits was sitting in the window. They are so cute. Their sharp little teeth will chew through a wire cord.

Straight ahead of him was kennel after kennel of dogs looking for a home. The howling got worse. There were also several cages holding baby kittens, but he didn't want a cat that would claw his furniture to death.

"Can I help you?" said a young girl who had stepped out of the back room. She was wearing a white smock over her good clothes, feeding a black baby kitten with an eye dropper.

"Yes. But first I want to take a good look at each dog cage and see if I see any dog I like."

Slowly he walked along in front of the cages, peering in and putting his fingers in to stroke their eager faces. Most of the dogs licked his fingers and wagged their tails. Several dogs began barking furiously, jumping up and down scratching at the doors of their cages. How to make a choice? They were all so cute. He went slowly down the aisle peering in at the dogs. Then he spotted a Jack Russell Terrier sitting in the corner of his cage, giving him the eye. The puppy jumped up and raced to the cage door barking furiously, wagging its tail and shaking its head back and forth.

"That one is good for chasing skunks, if you have any in your back yard among other things. It is lively, energetic and needs exercise. Do you like going for walks in the evening? They do. They are very intelligent. They sometimes appear on television. I have seen one belonging to the senior detective in Midsomer Murders, a British production on TVO. He steals the show."

"I have heard people tell me that about them. I have made up my mind. The Jack Russell it is. I haven't any cash on me, will you accept my Visa?"

"We prefer cash. But a debit card would do. How would you like to take your dog home? On a leash? Or buy a cage? By the way, all our animals have been spayed that we sell. They can't procreate. Does that bother you?"

"Not in the least. I will buy a leash." The woman went and got the excited puppy out of its cage. It wagged its tail and leaped around furiously in her arms. Clancy scooped him up, with the dog licking the back of his neck. The little dog, so excited, let out a hot stream of piss on the front of his jacket.

"Not my lucky day. Do you have a cloth to wipe this off?" pointing to his jacket.

"Yes, I'm so sorry. The dogs don't usually do that. But when they get overly excited, this happens. Here's one," and she handed it to him. Clancy sponged himself off and hoped that the stain would not show. But the smell would linger. He decided to take the dog home and then change his clothes. Nothing came easy in this life. There was no free lunch.

"I think that I will call him Jack."

"A good name. It is nice to think Jack has gone to a happy home."

The parrot started squawking again, 'Fuck off, fuck off.'

"A popular fellow," said Clancy nodding to the bird and left the shop happily with his new dog on a leash. He would leave the dog with a bowl of water in the backyard until he got home that evening.

* * * * *

On the way back to the office, Clancy stopped at the cigar shop on the corner for the local paper, the Mariposa News and Packet. He laid the paper out on his desk and read down through the headlines. "Nothing here on the Lang murder. We need some witnesses. We have got zip so far. We're getting to be like Toronto. Someone gets shot in a crowded nightclub surrounded by tons of people and no one sees anything. Maybe we should jog people's memory."

"That means contacting Mira again," piped up Greg. "She's acting like a cold potato towards us at the moment. Someone needs to warm her up. How about you, Clancy? You're the man of the hour. Whet her appetite. Throw something juicy into the pot. Take her out for a drink. Meet up at the Brewery Bay Bar and ask for her help, appeal to her higher self."

"You have a head for suggestions, Greg, for other people. Yes, I can do that. I'll offer her one drink otherwise she will drink me under the table.

"That's the spirit. Off you go."

Clancy put in a call to eat 'em alive Mira and was surprised when she picked up the phone. "Yes."

"I was wondering if you would do me the pleasure of meeting me for a Happy Hour drink to day down at Brewery Bay?"

"To what do I owe this pleasure?" Mira's voice was cool.

"I thought we could shoot the breeze about the Lang murder case. I need some input."

"Yes, I suppose that would be a good idea. See you there at five."

"It will be a pleasure." He ended the conversation.

* * * * *

With no phones ringing and the office relatively quiet, David decided to take his coffee break down the street at Apple Annie's. The coffee they made in the office was burnt tasting like it had been boiled to death. He hated drinking it.

He hoped to pick up some local gossip on the Lang murder case and also anything else that was going on. He had planned to enter the marathon swim on Lake Couchiching but it had been cancelled because of the heat and the algae, Lake Couchiching this particular weekend had a high content of E-coli.

The bistro looked busy with full tables at the front of the store and line ups at the counter. He stood in line until it was his turn to be served.

Cheerful and loquacious, Marybeth a single mother

with voluminous breasts straining her cranberry sweat shirt was standing behind the cash register taking orders.

"What can I do for you" asked Marybeth looking him up and down with a big broad smile on her face. "Do you need doing?" She arched one eyebrow. "I love a man in uniform. So sexy. Aren't you the one who is investigating the Dr. Lang murder case?"

David nodded. "I am one of the investigating officers."

"Well, I may have something interesting to tell you involving two of the main players." She licked her lips and leaned eagerly forward to speak "There was an incident in here several weeks ago. It was quite nasty. Are you interested?" She thrust her heavy bosom over the counter almost brushing up against David's chest.

"Yeh, fire away," said David trying to keep his eyes off her breasts and instead on her face like the true gentleman he was.

"Well Saturday morning around ten, two women came in for morning coffee. One of them was Brenda Lang, Dr. Lang's wife. She's kind of a stuck up type, and the other one was a pretty blonde in her late twenties both of them wearing track suits and running shoes."

"Have you seen the blonde before?"

"I have seen her in here with Dr. Lang some mornings quietly chatting away in a booth in the back. They looked like they were on a break from the office. They only stayed about fifteen minutes." David thought that could be only one other person. That must be Nurse Sweet.

David nodded for her to continue.

"They got their coffee here at the desk, one cappuccino and one Americano and then took them to a booth at the back. They spoke so low, it was hard to hear what they were saying. Then their voices got louder. I heard Brenda say, *'you've been fooling around with my husband. Keep your paws off him or there will be big trouble.'* And the blonde says *'No, I haven't.'* *'Liar'* says Brenda. And the blonde demands she take it back and apologize. Brenda is irate, *'You apologize to me you, you husband snatcher. I won't stand for it.'* And she jumped up and threw her cup of hot coffee all over the blonde. There was immediate pandemonium in the store, with this woman shrieking, '*I've been scalded*', and Brenda shouting, '*bitch, bitch.*' .All the other customers were staring at the two of them. It was a nasty little scene."

"Did she get badly burned?"

"No, but it was the shock of it. She had to go home immediately and change. Her outfit was ruined.

I walked over and told Brenda that that kind of behaviour was unacceptable and she was not welcomed in here. I have never seen anything like it. But there is always a first time. Now what do you make of that? Is that any help?" she gave David a big smile

"Interesting," said David. "Thank you for telling me."

"I hope that you come back again and again. We always try to help the police." and she gave him a beautiful smile.

"Will do."

Privately he thought that puts a different spin on things. Clancy would be glad to get this juicy little tidbit. Miss Sweet was not as innocent as she proclaimed to be. She had been meeting Dr. Lang on the side and Brenda had gotten wind of their clandestine meetings.

* * * * *

Clancy headed over to the Medical Arts Building to see if he could catch Nurse Sweet who was tidying up Dr. Lang's affairs. He had a slightly different opinion of her now that he had heard from David about the catfight in Apple Annie's. She wasn't the sweet young thing she had made herself out to be. There had been a little hanky panky going on between her and Dr. Lang, a married man, and Brenda had called her on it.

He buzzed Dr. Lang's office, 'Detective Murphy'. He heard the buzzer sound and let himself in. After he entered the office, he slammed the door shut. Then strode across the carpet to confront Miss Sweet who was lightly running a feather duster along the top of the empty book shelves. She looked surprised at his abruptness. It was not like him at all. He was acting very unfriendly. What put him in such a bad mood?

"It has come to my knowledge that you, Miss Sweet,

have not been as open and as forthcoming as you appear to be. You had more than a professional relationship with Dr. Lang. You lied. I could prosecute you for obstructing justice. You withheld valuable information." He stared hard at her.

"Why did you say that? She batted her big blue eyes up at him. I saw him occasionally for coffee. No big deal," said Miss Sweet blushing profusely to the roots of her hair.

"You left out a few details when I last spoke to you. You didn't mention being in a fight with Brenda Lang, his wife, at the coffee shop."

"Well it was rather embarrassing to say the least, what happened in front of a room full of people having morning coffee. What happened was probably spread all over town afterwards. I hate to be the subject of cheap gossip."

"You also have been seen several times in the Brewery Bay Bar after office hours with Dr. Lang."

"Who said so? Who has been squealing? Is that a crime to meet?"

"It puts things on a different level. It puts your relationship on a more intimate level with Dr. Lang."

"Yes," she conceded, stepping down from the stool, "We would occasionally meet. It was perfectly harmless. It was totally innocent. Brenda accused me of having designs on her husband."

Clancy stared hard at her. "She must have felt some grounds, some reason for coming to that conclusion. You don't pluck an idea like that out of thin air."

"I told her that it was an employer/employee relationship that was all, nothing more, nothing less."

"She didn't believe you, hence the fight. Am I correct? I'm curious, meeting Dr. Lang so often, what did you two talk about?"

"Personal things."

"Like what?" he demanded.

"I might as well tell you. You will soon find out. He told me that he was unhappy. He said he had married the wrong woman. He said that his marriage was a big mistake. He didn't realize how big the mistake was until after he married Brenda."

"Did he talk about a divorce?"

"Well how could he? There was alimony to think of and lawyers' fees to pay. He didn't have the cash because he was in debt up to his ears. This was his second marriage and it bothered him that he could fail at this one also. He had such high hopes for this second marriage after the failure of his first marriage. That's why he moved to Mariposa. He wanted a different lifestyle but things were not working out."

"What was not working out?"

"His marriage. Brenda wanted more and more things. She couldn't control her spending and she was drinking. He felt that she couldn't control her drinking. He realized that he had made a big mistake in marrying Brenda. She was too high maintenance. She spent every cent he had. They had no children and he wanted children. It was an unhappy marriage."

"So eventually, if you played your cards right, you might become the next Mrs. Lang?"

"No, no, that isn't true. It was nothing like that. We didn't get that far. But I did have feelings for him and I believed that he was sincere and that he had feelings for me. I believed the feelings were mutual. But we didn't act on them."

"Are you sure?"

"Yes, I wanted him to get a divorce before we became involved."

"Is that all? Is that the whole story? How could he get a divorce? Dr. Lang was mortgaged up to his eyeballs."

"Yes, that was true. He was deeply in debt, which was causing him a lot of stress. As a friend I listened to him. I did not advise him at all. I just listened."

"What else did he talk about?"

"This was about all I can tell you," she sighed.

"To be happy sometimes we have to cut our losses. Do you think that was what he had to do?"

"I urged him to be patient, to work things out. I did not want him to do anything other than what was good for him. I urged him to get counseling for his wife. Get her into an AA program. He said how embarrassing it was to be a professional psychiatrist and have a wife who is an alcoholic."

"Was that the last time you met?"

"Two days ago. In the office we kept strictly to office protocol."

"This might have had a great bearing on his murder, Miss Sweet, did you realize that?"

"No, I didn't."

"What if Dr. Lang told you that he had reconsidered and wanted reconciliation with his wife. That could be a motive for your killing him."

"No, no," cried Miss Sweet, with tears falling down her face. "It wasn't like that at all. That's a wicked thing to suggest. Wicked, wicked. You have spoiled my day. Please leave."

With that Clancy exited the office. She is one of my prime suspects never the less. She did have motive for murder. Brenda is the one she might have wanted to murder but not Dr. Lang. But what if Dr. Lang tried to back out of his relationship with Miss Sweet, what then?

* * * * *

The next person to interview was Brenda Lang to see what she had to say about the fight. He drove up the circular drive to the Lang residence. The drapes in the living room were closed. No lights were on. He noticed the grass needed cutting. Another car was parked to the side of the front door. He pulled in beside it. He didn't recognize it. He got out and headed for the front door. Just as he reached it, the door opened and Dr. Coldwater stepped out and headed for his car. His appearance at the widow's house looked very interesting.

"You make house calls?" he asked him.

"Yes, Mrs. Lang is my patient and she is having trouble sleeping. What is that to you?"

"Just inquiring."

He wondered why a pediatrician with a roomful of crying babies would drop everything to come over here during office hours and look after a widow who has trouble sleeping. Something funny was going on.

Clancy pressed the bell. On cue, the little dog could be heard yapping in the background, pawing the hard wood floors. He heard Mrs. Parker's footsteps. Then she opened the door.

"I have come to see Mrs. Lang."

"Have a seat in the living room while I go and fetch her."

He waited. Five minutes passed then ten. Mrs. Lang came slowly down the stairs to greet him. She looked disheveled. Her hair was messy and she had made no attempt to apply lipstick or make up. Her dressing gown fell open at the waist. He could see a pink nylon negligee underneath.

"I need a drink. You're working so I won't offer you one. I have got a migraine and it is getting worse. You keep coming here and asking me questions. I give you the same answers but you keep asking the same questions over and over again." She went over to the bar, picked up the decanter and poured herself a full glass. Then came and sat down beside him.

"I'm here to ask you about the fight you were in with Miss Sweet down at Apple Annie's."

"The bitch. Did she squeal to you about it?"

"The police have their sources. What was it about?"

"She had made moves on my husband. He was too naïve to see it, to see what she was up to, the scheming little cat. Men are so dumb. They can't recognize it even if it was put in front of their noses. I had heard from several people that she was meeting him socially for drinks at Brewery Bay and coffee at Apple Annie's. My husband was just being friendly, trying to be kind to her. He was trying to be charitable. But that wasn't her game plan. She was trying to steal my husband away from me. My husband loved me. We had many happy times together. We had our problems like any married couple but they were small problems. He loved me. He didn't love her, that piece of tail, that woman of no substance. She was after him from the get go. I decided to call her on it. So I went down there to have it out with her, to tell her to fuck off. I got carried away. I threw a cup of coffee on her," she shrugged her shoulders. "I couldn't help it. She denied everything. My marriage was at stake and I had to save my marriage." Her lip trembled. Tears were welling in her eyes. "I loved my husband. I was fighting to save my marriage."

Clancy reached for his handkerchief and pulled it out

of his pocket. He hoped it was clean and handed it to her. "Here, I am sorry if my questions are upsetting but they have to be asked."

Here was a motive. Brenda had motive to kill her husband if he was going to leave her, no matter what she said about him loving her. But where was the proof? Where was the evidence? He could not see the forest for the trees. He had nothing to go on. He drove back to the office and sat down at his desk to think.

* * * * *

Clancy was daydreaming when he heard Greg's voice. "Got something for you, Clancy. Dr. Lang's phone records."

"Finally some good news." Clancy noted the various numbers. From his residence he had made calls to; Dr. Coldwater's number, Dr. Knelman, in Toronto. But surprise, surprise, guess who was the last person he spoke with? Clancy knew without looking.

Back to the Medical Arts Building again to interview Miss Sweet to check out the latest clue .Miss Sweet seemed to be in this mess up to her eyeballs. She knew more than she was telling.

He buzzed to get in. No reply. He buzzed again. No answer. For ten minutes, he waited. A patient came out of the building on crutches and limped down the stairs. Clancy slipped in the door behind him. At suite 200, he rapped sharply on the door. He tried the door handle. The door was locked. That was strange. She was usually in during office hours. He went and found the super for the building, whose office was in the basement.

"Come and unlock the office door. I have some concerns," he said, flashing his badge. The super came up with him and unlocked the office door, and they went in. Piles of rubbish everywhere, wastebaskets full, but no Miss Sweet. Obviously she was not here. "How much longer is the office going to be open?" asked Clancy.

"They have a month extension," said the super.

Now where had Miss Sweet gone? Where could she be

found? He knew of a couple of places starting with Apple Annie's. He drove over to the cafe, and parked his car in front of it. He wandered in, noticing who were sitting in the front of the cafe near the window, some geriatrics with canes sitting with ladies with white puffed hair. Most of the customers were baby boomers with time to spare and not sure what to do with it. At leisure. Not all the time, a lot of them did volunteer work in the community which was much needed. He glanced up at the paintings hung above him. Strong warm colours, no pastel scenes of the countryside, of forests and streams. Just vigorous and violent.

Then he peered into the booths along the wall. No Miss Sweet. Finally at the back, huddled in a booth, almost out of sight was the unhappy Miss Sweet keeping her blonde head down, sipping coffee out of a large pottery mug. He strode towards her. "Miss Sweet, I called at your office but you weren't there."

She nodded. "I was taking a break. I needed some fresh air and to get away from the office."

"Mind if I sit down?"

"Suit yourself." He slipped into the seat opposite her.

"Miss Sweet our phone records show that you were the last person that Jerry Lang called on his cell phone before he was murdered. The time was 4 pm shortly before he was murdered. What was that about? Why did he call you instead of his wife, for instance? You were the last person to talk to him. From where I stand, this is incriminating evidence. Explain."

"I didn't think it was important to mention it. Dr. Lang wanted his favourite Mont Blanc pen that he had forgotten in the office. He wanted me to bring the pen down to him so that he would have it. It was his favourite pen."

"Where did he call from?' He knew the answer but he wanted to hear what she would say.

"He called from his house. I was just tidying up and got the call a few minutes before I was going to leave. He is not forgetful and I was surprised that he had forgotten his favourite pen."

"So you thought that getting his pen was just an excuse to talk to you."

Miss Sweet blushed.

"Am I right? You thought that he had something important he wanted to say to you other than getting his pen? Did he say anything to you, Miss Sweet, some excuse for speaking to you, some tender words of goodbye before leaving for the medical convention?"

"No, it was not like that. No like that at all." She blushed. "Yes, I did want him to say a few words to me before he left for his conference." She looked down at her hands, her fingers twisting around and around in her lap. "I never really got to say goodbye." She wiped a tear from the corner of her eye.

"What instructions did he give you?"

"I was to drive down the Concession Road and meet him where it intersects the trail. I did as he told me. I drove down and parked my car behind his Lexus. His car was in front of mine. I thought that he would be there looking for me and it would be just a simple exchange. But then all of a sudden another car drove up, a black SUV. I recognized the car. It was Brenda's and she was hopping mad. She slammed the car door and came rushing towards me. She swung her purse at my face and landed a punch on my jaw, all the time screaming at the top of her lungs, *'trying to run away with my husband, are you? I heard you on the phone. Think I am stupid, to all your antics.'* She had been listening to our conversation on the extension up at the house. She went on and on, half crazed. A real wild cat. I couldn't get a word in edgeways to explain about the pen. She almost knocked me to the ground with her pushing and shoving. I stumbled badly, almost fell trying to get away from her."

"Where was Dr. Lang?"

"He was nowhere in sight. The car was empty. He must have started out jogging."

"What did you do next?"

"I had to get away from her so I ran down towards the trail, in an effort to lose her and also to find Dr. Lang."

"Did she follow?"

"She was wearing running shoes but I was faster. I glanced behind but she had fallen back. I heard her shout that she would have me fired come Monday when Dr. Lang got back from the conference."

"Did you see anybody on the trail? Anybody at all?"

"No one at all."

"What happened next?"

"I waited a few minutes then I walked back, got back into my car and drove off."

"What about Brenda? Did you see her again?"

"No."

Was her car still there?"

"Yes."

"What did you do after that?"

"I drove home."

"Did you see anybody? Anyone that can verify your presence?"

"No one."

"This better be the truth, Miss Sweet or you will be booked for murder."

"It happened just as I told you. Why can't you believe me? I had nothing to do with his murder."

"I hope, for your sake and mine, Miss Sweet; it is as you told me. I hope you have left nothing out. There is a lot of information that you have held back. This investigation would have gone a lot smoother and faster if you had been more forthcoming." He got up from the booth, not at all happy with Miss Sweet and her new revelations. Every time he met up with her, there was a new story. He headed out.

* * * * *

The door flew open with a bang, just as Clancy bit his teeth into a nice, sugary maple doughnut. He put it down and wiped the crumbs from his lips. It was Mira in her black mini-skirt, holding her notebook and tape recorder. She strode in and flounced down in the chair in front of his desk.

"Got one for me? I bet you have. What a cheapskate you are. You pick my brains in the bar at Brewery Bay for the price of one beer. Give me a break. How cheap can you get? Or should I say how low can you go? Do you think you can buy off the press with one beer?" She slammed her notebook on this desk. "Payback time .and I am not buying you a beer. Your turn to cough up and don't go in circles, like the politicians, all talk and leading nowhere. I need something meaty."

"The way you come across, Mira, you'd think that there was nothing happening in this town at all that we were all idle layabouts. Plenty has been going on. I have been interviewing suspects endlessly since I last talked to you. I have narrowed it down to a handful of suspects."

"A handful? How did you arrive at that number? Did you consult a crystal ball?" Mira could be very sarcastic.

"It was a process of timely elimination, Mira. It was all painstakingly done. It took a lot of patience. We don't want to rush things and make a false arrest. Just like you do your work researching stories, we take a lot of time and care to arrive at certain conclusions."

"So what have you got? She crossed her legs so that he could almost see her crotch from where he was sitting. He glimpsed a pair of black lace panties.

"Let's put it this way, Mira. First we looked very carefully at those closest to him. Often the first suspects in any murder case are the immediate family. If it is not the immediate family, then there is someone next to him like a friend, associate or relative. Does that help? You can say the police are close to making an arrest in the Lang murder case. I can't tell you anything more than that. Maybe that will help us flush out the murderer if you put that in print."

"So I write that the police are close to making an arrest after a couple of months of investigation. Whoopee! That doesn't say a whole lot. I have got to regurgitate all the known facts and then end up with that one sentence?"

"That's about right, Mira."

"Put this in your pipe and smoke it. Don't think I am going to come across again for the price of one beer. You can find some other dope."

"Mira, I am so grateful for your help. I am just on a policeman's salary and I can't afford much."

"Yeh, well the word for you is cheap, cheap, cheap." She gathered up her things and flounced out.

"Well," said Greg," you certainly laid a charm on her."
"Get lost," said Clancy.

* * * * *

At 5 pm, Clancy made his way to Dr. Frost's house for some wine and cheese. Clancy's little social get together with Dr. Frost would soon prove to be too much for him. His migraine was throbbing at the side of his head from drinking too much red wine, when he staggered into the office the next morning. He had forgotten how allergic he was to red wine.

"What a red glow your nose has," exclaimed Greg looking up from his computer. "You are all lit up like Rudolph the red nose reindeer."

"How diplomatic you are. My aching head! Dr. Frost had me over last night to his place for a little wine and cheese after work. I spent Happy Hour at the coroner's place. I didn't want to go that much but it pays to be pals with the coroner. I drank some cheap red wine. Maybe it was expensive. I don't know and now this morning, I have come out in hives, big, red blotches all over my face, arms and torso. I have forgotten that I was allergic to red wine. I hardly ever drink the stuff but I couldn't turn down his invitation. It might look offensive."

Greg enviously said," you get no sympathy from me. I wish someone would invite me over to drink some hooch and taste some cheese. The game is called, Play and pay."

"What's the latest?"

"Around 11 pm last night a couple were making out down by the Trans Canada Trail. They had spread a blanket behind some bushes and were getting it on. There was a full moon. When they heard what they first thought were fire crackers going off. But then realized it was gun shots. They phoned 911. Next they looked around for where the shots came from. They found a youth lying on the trail path, writhing in agony with a bullet in his upper leg. Whoever shot him had run off.

"The hospital has phoned in accordance with police regulations that any gunshot wound has to be reported to the police. One of our suspects in the Lang murder case, your little weasel, the drug dealer, Jimmy Snipes is in the hospital with a gunshot wound to the upper thigh."

"Maybe I should go over there and pay him a visit, have a little bedside chat, Jimmy and me."

"Do you think that will make him feel better or worse?"

"Probably not better but a little information might be forthcoming from our chat as to who did it."

Clancy drove over to the hospital. The parking lot was almost full. He was tempted to park in the handicapped space which was available but then had second thoughts. He was travelling in a marked vehicle. The police have to set a good example to the community and he'd get no points for parking there. He walked towards the powered front doors which nicely opened for him as he approached. 'Wash your hands' dispensers were set up inside the door. He squeezed some disinfectant onto his hands and rubbed. Ahead of him, the smell of fresh coffee hit him from the Tim Horton's coffee stand set up in the lobby. He was dying for a cup but didn't have time to grab one.

At the Admissions Desk he asked the receptionist who wore a volunteer badge on her blazer, "Do you have a new patient named Jimmy Snipes?" She typed his named into her computer. "Yes admitted late last night. "Third floor, third door on your right."

He got into the elevator with an old geezer in a wheelchair and his elderly wife. When the elevator opened, before he could get out, the old geezer quickly rolled the wheelchair over his feet, 'sorry about that'. I bet you are, thought Clancy as he limped down to Snipes' room. The next thing that will happen, a nurse will drop a bedpan on my aching feet to really cripple me.

Jimmy with his leg in a pulley hanging from the ceiling was lying in the white hospital bed, looking very unhappy, like a man caught sitting on a toilet and his bowels not moving. He had spent the early morning hours in OR and now was trying to collect his thoughts which an anesthetic does a good job of erasing.

Clancy pulled up a chair to his bedside, careful not to bump the hospital bed which in fact he did.

"Ouch," shouted Jimmy still groggy from the anesthetic.

"Sorry about that. Had a little party on the trail last night, Jimmy? Do you want to tell me about it?"

"Yeh, sure. Not really, it was a deal gone bad. I almost got killed."

"That's nothing new for you, Jimmy. You are a big boy now. These things happen. This is part of the business. Eat and be eaten. Out with it. You might as well tell me as anyone."

"I'll do the best I can under the circumstances. I remember that I had my stuff ready, weighed in a plastic bag that I kept in the trunk of my car for a buyer who wanted to buy some pot for medicinal reasons for his mother's cancer. You are allowed to sell pot for medicinal purposes."

"Oh sure," said Clancy, "Medicinal pot for his mother, oh please spare me that excuse."

"Yeh, that's what he said. So we shook hands on the deal and I went to get the bag out of the trunk of my car parked on Concession Road. He followed me. Then he pulled a gun on me and said he wasn't going to pay. I said, this is not the way we do business, put the gun away."

"Who was he? Come on, you know who he was."

"Never saw him before in my life. Honest!" Jimmy threw up his hands. "He was just another anonymous contact. Anyway, another guy jumps out from behind a parked car and joins this guy with the gun. I struggle with the guy with the gun, the gun goes off and I get a bullet in my thigh. They run off with my bag of pot. Somebody nearby on the trail hears the shots ring out and calls 911. An ambulance arrives and here I am. I could have been dead if the bullet had entered higher up."

"What a difference a few inches makes. Poor you." Clancy glanced around the room taking everything in. He spied a little red telephone address book sitting on top of the bedside table. He reached for it.

"Hey, that's my private property. You can't take that." Jimmy struggled to move but couldn't. He was in a body cast and his damaged leg was held high in the air by a pulley.

"Borrow is the word, Jimmy, borrow."

"You need a search warrant for that."

"This little book will be treated with the utmost respect and care. Just lie back on your pillow and relax."

"You're taking advantage of a disabled man."

"I bet in this little book you have some of Dr. Lang's patients as clients, I bet you do." Humming he thumbed his way through the index. "Holly Jones. That's an interesting name, the lawyer's wife, to have in there. What do you two have in common?"

"I wouldn't know."

"When did you last see her?"

"A while ago. Friday 13th. I was getting out of my car to call on her."

"What time? "

"Midafternoon around three. She was backing out of her driveway. She was in such a hurry she didn't realize that I was there. So I followed her in my car, hoping to catch up with her. She headed down to the lake. When she turned a corner, she was going so fast, she ran over a squirrel, which became road kill. I lost her on the corner."

"Did you know where she was heading?"

"Nope. Her car was gone when I rounded the corner at the intersection one street up from the lake."

"Well Jimmy, I am borrowing your little book and I will return it when I am finished."

"You can't do that."

"Oh yes, I can. Jimmy. Lie back on the pillow and count sheep"

Jimmy yelled, "Nurse, nurse."

"Jimmy, there are too many guys in here screaming nurse, nurse for her to drop everything and come running to you. Too many patients want the bed pan. Get real." And Clancy sauntered out the door pleased with his little find.

* * * * *

Clancy decided to check in at the office before interviewing Mrs. Lang again. It was hard going. He walked into the office. His two colleagues had their heads down looking very busy. "In all this mess, it's hard to find a place to sit down." complained Clancy clearing some paper away from his desk. "What is the public going to think?"

David looked up, "Testy, testy. Don't be testy."

Mrs. Holly Johnson in a low cut frilly white blouse bolero style and black Spanish Capri's, with a dangling silver charm bracelet on her tanned arm, wobbled into the office on her straw wedges.

Appearing busy, Greg was sitting at the reception desk shuffling through some papers, mostly gas receipts. She bent over so that he could get an eyeful of her assets and asked demurely. "May I speak with Detective Clancy Murphy, please?"

"What about madam?" said Greg, smacking his lips. "He is pretty busy these days. Anything lost or stolen I can handle it."

"I am sure you can. My concerns are about the murder investigation."

Greg got up and went back to Clancy's office. "Clancy, there is a lady who would like to speak to you about the murder investigation. She has some nice knockers on her."

"In that case, I will be right out."

What brings her here he thought when he saw it was Mrs. Jones, It's a little far from her usual playground.

"Mrs. Jones, how can I help you? We have talked before."

"It's making me nervous living in this town with a killer running loose. Have you made any progress? I need some reassurances. I am home alone a lot and my husband is away in Barrie."

"You surprise me, Mrs. Jones," He gave her a hard stare;" You don't seem to be the nervous type."

Mrs. Jones didn't even blink an eye. "I hate to disappoint you but I am. My nerves are bad." And she drummed her long red fingernails on his desk.

"We are progressing .slowly. But it takes time. We want all of our i's dotted and t's crossed. We can't afford to arrest the wrong person and then get slammed with a false arrest suit. We will keep you informed."

"Are all of Dr. Lang's patients suspects?"
"Everyone is a suspect."
"I see and that includes me, does it?"
"Yes, until such time you are eliminated. You have no alibi for that time."
"Well that's not very hopeful or helpful."
Clancy raised his hands. "It's the best I can do, Madam."
"That's not good enough." With that Mrs. Jones turned and flounced out of the office.
"What did I tell you," announced Greg," isn't she something else? I'd like to get my hot little hands on her."
"Yeh, well she's deadly. Her husband is a lawyer and lawyers like to sue."
"Thanks for the tip. It appears to be look but don't touch."

* * * * *

"I am sitting on the phone while you lot are out and about." said David, "I just had a call and pleased to say that we finally got a witness around the time Dr. Lang was murdered. A senior, Mr. Henry Hunter, was out for an afternoon drive down by the lake. He's retired and has some spare time on his hands. He drove down Concession Road and saw two cars parked near the trail, a silver Lexus and behind it a black SUV .parked a short distance away from the other. How long were they parked there? He couldn't say. It was June 19th and it just now jogged his memory that this information could be important for the police in solving the case. There was nobody in the cars, they both were empty. People had gone for a short stroll. That is what he thought."

"He didn't mention a red Ford did he? The one that Miss Sweet drives?"

"No, they were the only two cars he saw. He wasn't paying that much attention. He didn't think it was important."

"Mm, it sounds like this was in the time frame after Miss Sweet left if her car wasn't there. Clancy took out a biro and wrote down the details. "I am going to call on Mrs. Lang.

She owns a black SUV. See what she has to say."

He phoned the Lang residence. Mrs. Parker answered.

"I have to ask Mrs. Lang some more questions. I will be over there in fifteen minutes."

Clancy drove up the familiar driveway. Again he noticed Dr. Coldwater's car parked to the side of the front door. He seems to be a frequent visitor here. He rang the bell. He heard the familiar yap, yap of the little dog. Mrs. Parker opened the door.

Clancy took off his hat and nodded. "Mrs. Parker I want to speak to Mrs. Lang. Will you get her for me?"

"Dr. Coldwater is seeing her now. He will be down in a few minutes. He is just leaving. Bear with me. She's having trouble sleeping at night,"

Just then, Dr. Coldwater thumped his way down the front stairs gripping his black leather medical bag.

"Hello Dr. Coldwater. You seem to be a frequent visitor here. Are you seeing Mrs. Lang professionally? I thought your specialty was pediatrics. My mistake."

"Yes, "said Dr. Coldwater, "and as for the rest of your questions, none of your damn business. I cite patient confidentiality." He breezed past him and then opened the front door before slamming it shut.

Mrs. Lang, her hair tousled, with no makeup on, her shaky fingers holding a lighted cigarette, came slowly down the stairs. Every movement she made could be seen in the pain on her face. She slid into a chair. "You again." She sighed. "Will it never end? I don't know how much more questioning I can take."

"I won't sit down, Mrs. Lang, but there are some urgent questions that I have got to have answers to, Mrs. Lang."

Now, getting back to Friday 19th around 4 pm. You had another fight with Miss Sweet, near the Cross Canada Trail. Miss Sweet said she eventually left and when she walked to her car, your car was still there. You were alone down there. Did you manage to meet up with Dr. Lang? This is a very important question for you to answer, Mrs. Lang. Take your time in answering it." He starred hard at her.

Mrs. Lang appeared on the verge to collapse. She sank

into the nearest chair, her hands trembling. "I waited and waited but he had gone jogging. He didn't take his cell phone with him. The trail was devoid of any other person."

"Did you see anyone? Anyone at all?"

She paused, with a faraway look on her face. "I am trying to think." He waited for her to reply. She lifted her head and looked at him. "Yes, yes. As I stood there I did see one other person, a tall slim woman jogger going by as she rushed by down the trail. I did not get a good look at her."

Clancy felt a tingling at the back of his neck. "Describe her. What was she wearing?"

"A powder blue jumpsuit, black granny bag around her waist and pink and white trainers."

"What colour was her hair?"

"Brunette. She was wearing it in a ponytail

"Did you recognize her?"

"I only saw the back of her head. She could have been a patient. She could have been anyone."

"So you have no idea who this woman is to give you an alibi?"

"She was tall for a woman, 5.7. She looked very fit and trim, athletic, and anxious to get away."

"Did you notice anything else?"

"I thought it a bit strange, but she had bits of leaves on her track pants, as If she had been rolling in the leaves."

"Do you remember who that person was? Was she a patient of Dr. Lang's?"

"I have no idea." She shook her head. "No idea at all."

"Try and refresh your memory and in the meantime, I will be doing some investigation as to who this other person was. You're a prime suspect, Mrs. Lang. Think of something that will clear your name." He let himself out.

* * * * *

"An incoming call." Greg announced. "We have Dr. Coldwater on the line. He sounds like he could eat you alive or bite you on the rear."

What a pain thought Clancy picking up the phone.

What has got his shorts in a knot? "Detective Clancy, here."

"My patient, Brenda Lang has been having a problem lately affecting her health. It has been acerbated by your constant questioning of her. You haven't arrested her but you keep on going to her house and harassing her, trying to intimidate her. She is a high strung woman, of nervous condition, has trouble sleeping and is in my professional opinion on the verge of a nervous breakdown if you keep this up. Anything can push her over the edge. I am insisting that the next time, you want to question her, that I be present. Those are doctor's orders. This harassment cannot continue. Do I make myself clear?"

"Yes and no. I am trying to solve a murder case which involves the killing of her husband, your friend. I am trying to find out who did it and it seems everyone is trying to obstruct me in carrying out my duties."

"Tough beans," replied Dr. Coldwater." I will not have it. She can only be seen in my presence. Do I make myself clear? Or do you want it in writing?"

"My mandate is to investigate a murder. I have to take whatever steps are necessary."

"Make sure you don't overstep your mandate." He slammed the phone down. I must be getting close, thought Clancy.

* * * * *

There was one tall woman, that he could think of with brunette hair in a ponytail, slim and athletic, a patient of Dr. Lang's, Mrs. Holly Jones. It might be just a coincidence, maybe. He didn't know for sure. It was a hunch, a strong hunch. His gut feeling told him that he was right.

He called her on her cell phone. He was surprised to find her picking it up. "I have more questions to ask you, Mrs. Jones."

"If you call here more often my husband will get ideas. He will think we are having an affair."

"I'm a married man," he reminded her, "and I don't nibble."

"You gave me the impression that you did. What a mistake I made." She tried to sound apologetic but a little laugh gave her away.

Was she smoking pot already?

"I have some serious questions to ask. Will you be in?"

"Yes, I will be in," she sighed," maybe you can share a martini with me."

"I'll be there in ten minutes."

He drove up the circular driveway and knocked on the door several times. No answer. He looked through the window to see if anyone was around. The house appeared vacant. She said that she would be in. He glanced over at the pool gate. She likes to swim in the afternoon. I'll try that door. He knocked, this time with more success.

Holly opened the gate door wearing a long nylon and silk robe which separated at the front to reveal her bare feet. "Just taking a little swim, doing some lengths in the pool. I like to swim naked. It's good for the soul. I like communing with nature. I am not ashamed of my body. So many people are."

"An eye full for the neighbours, no doubt. You jog, don't you, as well as swim?"

She didn't beat around the bush. "Yes, that's true,"

"May I sit down? I have some questions to put to you. You were out on the Trans Canada Trail Friday, June 13th, weren't you? We have a witness who says they saw you there." This was a lie because the witness could only give a physical description and he did not yet have the confirmed identity of the female jogger. This was a stab in the dark. He wanted to see how she would react to his question. It was a wild guess.

She ran her finger along the side of her neck. "That's a little while ago. I may have been. I didn't say I wasn't on the trail. Yes, I was there as I recall." She sounded cagey, on the defensive.

"You knew that Dr. Lang would be there. Most of his patients knew he jogged at that time. Did you bump into Dr. Lang on the trail? He was on the trail at the same time as you were on it. First tell me what you wanted from him?"

Holly arched her eyebrows. "I was on the trail, and I did

not meet up with him. You can believe me or not believe me. That is your choice. I know what you are getting at. I am telling you the truth. Don't try to frame me for something I didn't do. Do I need my husband's presence as my lawyer?"

"But you were there and he was killed close to the spot that you jogged by."

"You can't pin this on me. I had nothing to do with it. That's all coincidental, that he was there the same time as I was."

"You wanted to meet up with him whether he wanted to or not."

"That's kind of harsh for you to say."

"You felt you were in love with him."

"I had a crush on him," she stretched out her legs and uncrossed them, admiring her nice tan," like most of his women patients. Is that a crime?"

"Yeh, and it was going nowhere so you decided to do something about it so you went to meet him. Did you kill him?"

"I admit to wanting to meet him but he wasn't there I told you. I waited around hoping to bump into him either on the way to his car or on the way away from his car."

"How long?"

"About ten or fifteen minutes or so."

"Someone is lying." He stared at her. "Did you pass anyone on the trail?"

"As a matter of fact I did. I passed a woman who was down there, but in a hurry to rush off. Her car was parked on Concession Road behind his Lexus."

"What kind of car?"

"A black SUV."

Clancy thought, this confirms Brenda Lang's story so far.

"What was she doing?"

"I didn't pay close attention. She was running to her car."

"What was she wearing? Was she blonde or brunette?"

"It's a blur. It's too long ago. Her hair was blonde. I think. She was dressed in pink, in a pink sweat suit. She was in her late thirties."

"Have you seen her before?"

"No, I don't recall."

"Did you see anybody else?"

Mrs. Jones shook her head.

"What did you do after that?"

"I went looking for Dr. Lang on the trail. The woman was of no interest to me. So I continued jogging. I didn't find him."

"What conclusion did you come to?"

"His car was there, his Lexus on Concession Road, so I must have missed him somehow. I went home and had a shower, got into some comfortable clothes and had a Martini."

"That's all you can tell me. That's all that happened?"

"Yes. I have told you everything. You can ask me the same questions over and over again and you will get the same answers. I need a drink. Will you join me?"

"I will take a rain check. Be on standby Mrs. Jones for further questions. Things are heating up." And he let himself out.

* * * * *

Back at the office at his desk, Clancy settled himself in comfortably. Then he took out a white pad out of his drawer and drew a triangle. Three women wanted Dr. Lang and who loved him. One of them did it. Which one? Whose story did he believe?

How can I think about what Holly Jones has just told me? How can I concentrate? This place is a mess. The garbage can is full of apple cores, Tim Horton cups and greasy serviettes. Flying all over my desk are memos with "**URGENT**" printed in red. Who to call first? I am right on the cusp of solving the Lang murder case and can't get through the forest for the trees with this pile up of debris. Mrs. Lang didn't leave when she said she did or Mrs. Jones is lying. It's a tossup. I need some direction, some inspiration. Maybe if I get out of the office and get some fresh air. It will be good for my brain cells.

Two p.m. it was time for a late lunch. He thought of French's that cute little yellow wooden shack at the edge of the park that sold hotdogs and hamburgers with fries, overlooking the marina and Lake Couchiching. Children played in the playground's jungle gym watched over by their mothers. On the grass, people were sitting on blankets eating their paper bag lunches. The odd cyclist whipped by on the boardwalk, scaring the walkers who had to shift to one side to allow him to pass.

The lake was a beautiful blue today, the water calm and inviting. The sunshine sparkled on the water's surface like diamonds. It was a very restful place to pause and enjoy the sun and the outdoors.

French's had been there for years, Stephen Leacock had his afternoon tea there according to a little bronze plaque on one of the outdoor tables in the 1920 to1940s Imagine Leacock drinking tea? He named the location of his summer home, on the lake Brewery Bay and was known to be fond of the hard stuff.

He drove over, parked his car and then stepped up to the counter and ordered a hamburger with fries and root beer. He was waiting for his order when he recognized the man standing behind him. Eric Badas. He nodded. Badas smiled. "I have a tip for you, favour for favour. Since you didn't book me for that fight in the pool hall. I owe you one."

"That's nice to hear. Spin away."

"Yeh, well at the fire station we have been getting false alarms about a fire at the Holly Jones residence. We had one last week. We get over there and we check everything out but there is no fire. Mrs. Jones cigarette may have set off the fire alarm. She was a bit high when we got there. The smell of pot was in the air throughout the downstairs rooms. It is a complete waste of tax payer's money and time for us to follow up on these false alarms. Every call we make we have to notify the insurance company. The insurance companies don't like it. She is all apologetic about it. But I think it is a ruse to get us over there. She's bored and wants attention or else she is high on weed. We warned her, the next time she will be fined. Just thought you might want to know"

Clancy thanked him, "I'll file that away. Don't worry I will act on it."

"Your order is ready." Clancy picked up the paper bag and sat down at a picnic table in the sunshine. So much for the diet he was suppose to be on for his high cholesterol. He was taking Lipitor like half the town to clean out his clogged arteries. He usually ate like a rabbit boring things like carrot sticks, cucumbers, radishes, lettuce and tomatoes. But today was an exception.

* * * * *

Once back at the office, the phone started ringing. "For you," yelled out Greg," the caller sounds like a mad pit bull in a china shop, snarling and pawing on its chain." He handed the phone over to Clancy.

"OPP, Detective Clancy Murphy, here."

"This is Hugh Jones, lawyer and husband of Holly Jones. You remember me. We spoke already on the phone. Although we have never met, you have called me in Barrie. You and I have a big problem. Too many times you have come over to our house to interview my wife. You have been asking too many questions. Is this professional interest or have you got the hots for my wife? You have gone over there too many times on fishing expeditions. Is my wife a suspect in the Jerry Lang murder case, or isn't she? I want an answer right now? If she is, I want to have a lawyer there and make sure that she only answers your questions in his presence."

"Everyone is a suspect. It's a process of elimination," said Clancy mildly.

"Well that's not good enough. I have a cynical mind, Detective Murphy. You wouldn't be using these visits as a weak excuse for pressing your advances on my wife, would you?"

"How dare you. I am only doing my professional duty. I am investigating a murder case," snapped Clancy

"Well it's my job to protect my wife from your fishing expeditions. She is being hounded and harassed and I won't stand for it. If you keep this up, I will lay charges of police harassment against you. I will go right to the top. I play golf with the commander in chief of your station, over in Barrie."

"Don't try to intimidate me, threaten me with a lawsuit. I am just trying to do my job and eliminate suspects. Your wife was seen down on the Trans Canada Trail around the time Dr. Lang was killed. That makes her a suspect. If she didn't do it, she has nothing to worry about."

"I am not threatening you. I am just telling you, leave my wife alone."

"Be careful, that your wife and you don't get charged with obstruction of justice."

"You're the one who should be careful," and he slammed down the phone.

"I'm not popular in some quarters. That was Mr. Hugh Jones blowing in my ear. As a lawyer, he feels he can intimidate the police and that he has every right to do so. He'll learn the hard way."

Greg said, "Go easy on that one. He has connections with the higher ups."

"Yeh, he told me that too. Irritating bastard. Now I must get back to whatever I was doing." Clancy sighed. "He got me so riled up, now I have just forgotten what I was doing."

* * * * *

It was hot. So hot he could hardly think. He needed a cold one and he thought of the waterfront down by the lake, with its cool breezes blowing off Lake Couchiching. He thought of the Legion Hall where he could sit outside on the patio or inside with the air conditioning on. Thelma, the retired nurse, would probably be on bar duty in the afternoons. He had a sentimental attachment to this place. The name of his uncle who served in World War II, was engraved on the pillar outside the building with the other names of veterans. He had never returned, a young boy of 19, just out of high school, who died, so keen to do his bit for his country. He liked to run his finger over the name. Anybody could join the legion. It was open to all. You didn't need to be a veteran.

He climbed the stairs and went in. The room was dark. The lights had been turned off to keep the room cool. He looked around. There was hardly anybody here. A couple of old veterans in their eighties sitting by the window stared back at him.

Thelma put down her crossword puzzle. "Hi, how can I help you?"

"I need a cold one. How about Labatt's Blue?"

"Coming right up." She snapped off the bottle cap and handed the bottle to him along with a glass.

He took the cold beer and went over to a table in front of the large plate glass window overlooking the lake. On the docks, the Mariposa Belle was out of its slip sailing on the lake.

He took a slow sip. It was time to think.

The eternal triangle. He figured that this was where he should concentrate his efforts. Three women loved Dr. Lang. Brenda, Miss Sweet and Holly Jones. These are the three women I know of. There may have been others. Doctors have a certain aura about them like honey to the bees. All three women are present at the scene or close to where and when he was murdered. Which one did it?

We have a man out for a casual drive who sees the Black Sub parked on the road not far from the Lexus, He does not see any red Ford which means that Miss Sweet is gone from the scene. That leaves Brenda with about twenty minutes which she has not accounted for from the time the fight with Miss Sweet ended until the time she headed for her car.

Brenda says she saw a female jogger. Holly Jones, who was last on the scene, hanging around in hopes of seeing Dr. Lang for fifteen to twenty minutes, doesn't see anybody else except the back of a blond haired woman returning to her black sub.

Two people are in the same time frame, Holly Jones and Brenda Lang. Which one is lying? He thought he knew the answer. He picked up his cell phone.

It was time to give Dr. Coldwater a call. He dialed Dr. Coldwater's office. The secretary answered and curtly told him that Dr. Coldwater was with a patient and very busy. In the background he could hear the crying and sneezing. "He has a roomful of patients waiting for his attention. Your request will have to wait."

"Tell him I am heading over to Mrs. Lang's to ask more questions."

He hung up the phone and prepared to go. This was not going to be easy he thought. He drove up the driveway and parked his car. Then went to the door and pushed the bell. Mrs. Parker opened it.

"I have come to see Mrs. Lang."

"She has slept in this morning. I haven't seen her so far. I will go up and tell her that you are here. It may take a few minutes."

Mrs. Parker slowly lumbered up the long winding staircase. "The stairs are hard for me with my arthritis," and knocked on the bedroom door, with the little dog, yapping at her heels. "That's funny. She is not answering. She must be still asleep. I will go in and wake her." The dog followed her in, yapping loudly.

"Mrs. Lang. Mrs. Lang. Detective Murphy wants to see you downstairs." She shook the woman's shoulders. "Brenda, it's time to get up. Someone's here to see you." Brenda's slack body fell back into the bed like a dead weight. Mrs. Parker ran back to the top of the stars to yell down at Clancy. "I am getting no response from her when I shake her to awaken her."

Clancy took the stairs two steps at a time and dashed into the room. He checked her vital signs, slow pulse. He lifted one eyelid. Her pupil was dilated. Drugs. "She's breathing but just barely. Call 911 and get an ambulance here quick. She may have taken an overdose of sleeping pills. Accidentally or deliberately, it's hard to tell."

Then the doorbell rang. It was an angry Dr. Coldwater who let himself in. Seeing no one in the living room and hearing voices, he bounded up the stairs and into the bedroom. He glanced around the room taking in the scene of the comatose Mrs. Lang lying stretched out on the bed in front of him. He reached for her wrist and took her pulse. "Her pulse is very weak." Then he pushed back an eyelid. He walked over to the bedside table and grabbed the empty pill bottle. "She is in a drug induced coma. I don't know how many were left and how many she has taken. She has swallowed the rest of the bottle. I knew your questioning would push her over the edge. You have a lot to answer for. If she dies, I will hold you responsible for harassing my patient to death. Have you called the ambulance?"

"Yes I have."

Looking around the room he said, "I see an envelope over there, addressed to you propped up against the mirror."

Clancy picked up the envelope and tore it open. Inside the note read, *Life is not worth living without my husband. I did not kill him.*

"I can guess what is in the note," glared Dr. Coldwater.

Clancy stood there by her bedside, embarrassed and tight lipped until the ambulance crew came rushing up the stairs. Dr. Coldwater followed them out the door. "I will accompany the ambulance to the hospital to make sure she gets the best of care." His last words going out the door were, "if she dies I hold you responsible."

Clancy went back to the office, thinking what a mess. Coldwater was going to have his hide. He sat down in his chair to try to figure out what to do.

"Well how did it go?" asked Greg eager to hear the news.

"It didn't. I figured out who did it and when I went to arrest that person, Brenda Lang, had taken an overdose. We got her to the hospital. Will she make it? Hard to say. She left a farewell note saying, she didn't do it."

What a mess. The unhappy Mrs. Lang, who feared her husband, was leaving her for Miss Sweet, had attempted suicide.

"I figured that the person with the most to lose was Brenda Lang. One way or another Dr. Lang would have left her for Miss Sweet."

If she didn't do it, who did?

* * * * *

The radio crackled. A house fire. He listened to the dispatch waiting to catch the address, 30 Driftwood Drive.

The Jones residence. He got to his feet, threw on his jacket. He would follow the fire truck there and if it was another false alarm, he would book her. He grabbed the search warrant off the desk. He would search for drugs using this as an excuse to get her behind bars. Rushing outside, he caught a fleeting glance of Badas hanging for dear life to a pole on the back of the truck. Badas's winked at him, as if to say, what did I tell you, probably another false alarm.

The fire truck roared through the street. He turned on the siren, straight through the heart of town with people on the sidewalk gawping at the spectacle. A fire always gets them excited. The truck made a quick turn into the driveway and parked. Three firemen with axes headed for the front door just as the door flew open. Mrs. Jones in a flimsy silk housecoat and bare feet was standing just inside.

"There's no fire here," she said.

Ignoring her, the firemen brushed past her, followed by Clancy. "Where is it? Where's the fire? Your fire alarm sounded at our station."

He sniffed the air. It wasn't smoke. It was weed. Her cigarette had set it off. She made a vague gesture towards the den. "What fire? The smoke detector went off and I have no way of turning it off."

The men looked up at the ceiling where the whirring noise was still going on. "What set it off? Any idea?"

"No idea, she shrugged her shoulders, "no idea at all."

The chief turned to her. "Mrs. Jones, we warned you about false alarms. We have come to your house too many times for false alarms wasting our time and endangering the citizens of Mariposa. I have to make out a report. There will be a stiff fine and jail time. Your cigarette smoke set it off."

Clancy looked around. "It has got to be here somewhere." He started sifting through the clutter around her chair, the magazines and paperbacks. Then went over to the sofa and probed behind the cushions. He found it wedged down between two large cushions. "Aha! Here it is. There is enough here to book you on procession and trafficking." He held the clear plastic bag high in the air so that all could see. "Mrs. Jones, I am arresting you on drug charges and making too many false fire alarms. Hold out your hands."

"Since when has smoking pot in my own house become a criminal act?"

"It's the amount in your procession and the fact that you set off false fire alarms. Come along now," and he snapped the cuffs on her wrists.

"This is really too much, treating me like a common criminal. I have my rights. I won't answer another question until my lawyer gets here."

"Come along quietly so you won't disturb the neighbours."

"Fuck the neighbours." She lifted her foot to kick him in the balls but he was faster, he shoved her down in time into the cruiser.

"You can phone your lawyer down at the station. You get one phone call. Mind your head." What a bitch, he thought. I might have to call for reinforcement if she keeps this up. When they got back to the station, she was still yelling, "I am innocent. I am innocent."

Let her cool off in a cell for a few hours while her lawyer tries to get bail. Or until she thinks she will get bail. I will oppose it. I have a little surprise in store for her.

"In here." He led her into the office. "I want to speak to my lawyer," she was screaming." This place is filthy. I have my rights, you creep."

"Here's the phone. Make it snappy."

"Hugh, I have been falsely arrested. Get me out of here." She slammed down the phone. "That was short. It's time for lock up. Will you go quietly or do I have to drag you in there?" He took her down the hall to a holding cell and locked her in. Then he went back to his desk. He could hear her screaming, "I am innocent," over and over again." A little paper work was in order. Half hour later, a very angry red faced Hugh Jones was standing in front of him, his face lowered to meet his. A face uglier than a bull dog's.

"What have you done to my wife, you incompetent little creep?"

"I have locked her up for drug possession and setting off too many false fire alarms."

"I want her out on bail immediately and the charges dropped."

"It's up to the judge. She'll have to stay here overnight unless there is an evening bail hearing over in Barrie."

"I want bail as soon as possible."

"There may be a little difficulty."

"Why is that?"

"She's my prime suspect in the Jerry Lang murder case."

"Huh?"

"You heard me. She is my prime suspect. We have a couple of witnesses who place her at the scene of the crime."

Hugh leaned over his desk, a purple vein popping out in his forehead. "When I get through with you and your pitiful investigations and pathetic attempts to solve that murder, you won't have a job. Do you hear me?"

"Shouting and making personal remarks won't get you anywhere." Just then David walked over. "Do you need my help?'

"No, I can handle this myself. Mr. Jones was just about to leave."

Mr. Jones picked up his briefcase and slammed the office door after him.

*****

Just as he exited, Mira from the Mariposa Packet and Times rushed in, almost knocking Hugh Jones down. "Excuse me," roared Hugh Jones. "No problem," said Mira giggling and headed to the chair to sit down in front of Clancy. Mira was wearing a bright red blouse cut in a deep V down to the top of her breasts and her black miniskirt was thigh high almost level to her crotch. Nothing was left to the imagination. She leaned over his desk towards him.

"Clancy, you have been holding out on me. I have just been given a hot tip from one of your minions."

"Who squealed?" said Clancy with pursed lips.

"There's nothing private around here. I just bumped into Greg, your colleague, on the sidewalk outside the coffee shop. He was going in there to load up on doughnuts. Our paths crossed. Greg is no squealer but gradually, very gradually he let me pick his brains. Greg is never good under pressure. He quickly caved in. He melts like chocolate."

"What did you promise him in return? A leg over, Mira?"

"Maybe yes and maybe no. Just call it pillow talk. One way or another I will get the scoop."

"Mira, you and that paper of yours have tunnel vision."

"A job is a job and my duty is to report the news. Your job is to catch crooks. So tell me who have you got behind bars? I don't think it is your usual drunk, or drug pusher. Is it someone I know? And for what reason? This had better be good or your head will be on a platter"

"Holly Jones has been arrested on drug possession and setting off too many false fire alarms. Further charges are pending."

"My, my, that is interesting news for once. I smoke a little pot myself but you have never arrested me," smirked Mira, thrusting her big breasts out at him. "You have never laid a hand on me."

"I have never caught you at it. Don't think for a moment I wouldn't."

"Don't be a little toughie," she cooed. "Give me the details. The devil is in the details."

"By being arrested for pot possession and setting off false fire alarms, Holly Jones has breached her probation." He proceeded to give her the facts.

"False fire alarms set off by smoking pot. That would make a good headline. Further interest is captured by opening paragraph such as prominent lawyer's wife sets off false fire alarms by smoking pot. How does that grab you?"

"Not bad, Mira. Not bad. But we're having a little trouble with her husband, the lawyer, at the moment. He is threatening to sue for false arrest and anything else he can think of. The situation is iffy, as they say. Further charges are pending on a related matter, but I can't disclose that at this point until all our t's are crossed."

"You've got my attention," said Mira. "I guess this

information will have to do for now." She got up to leave, her skirt barely covering her ass. She slowly hitched it down. "Don't hold back on anything, Clancy, or I'll fry you in oil."

"How sweet you are, Mira. How very sweet," said Clancy glad to get rid of her. The person he would like to fry in oil was that big squealer, Greg. He is as weak as water. Why can't he learn that Mira is not to be trusted, not to be told anything?

* * * * *

Miss Temple got up from her nap, went into the kitchen and put the kettle on, and took the biscuit tin with the Queen's picture on it, down from the shelf. When the kettle had boiled, she let the tea bag steep first in the teapot before she poured herself a nice cup of tea. After tea she got ready to go out. She pulled up her black cotton knee highs and made sure the laces on her shoes were tied properly. She couldn't afford another fall. Her poor old head wouldn't take it. The elastic on her pantaloons was good, no need to worry there about them falling down. She pulled down on the hem of her cotton dress, so that it covered her knees. She was going out to do an errand, something she intended to do for a long time.

Greg was looking out the front window of the OPP office when he spied her, an old lady with white hair, dressed in black coming along the sidewalk. "Oh migawd, it's Miss Temple outside, coming in to pay us a call. I am going to the toilet and lock myself in. Knock on the door when she's gone."

"Thanks, pal, as if a visit from Hugh Jones and Myra weren't enough today." said Clancy

Miss Temple trotted in and stood with a determined look on her face in front of the main counter.

"Yes?" said Clancy hesitantly looking over the counter at her.

"I have come to thank you for finding my purse and returning it to me. All my ID were safe and sound. It was a great help to me. I have been in the hospital for several weeks and this is why I have not been able to get over here. I have got all my marbles despite being hit on the head.

I have come today to enquire how the investigation is going into the attempted break in at my cottage a while ago. I hope you remember. You and another person came to my house and took notes that night. Several months have passed and I have received no word. Have you caught anybody? Have you any suspects in mind?"

"My dear lady," said Clancy reaching out to pat her on the hand.

Miss Temple stepped back. "I am nobody's *dear*. I will have you know."

"Please forgive me," said Clancy. "You remind me so much of my dear mother who passed to the other side over ten years ago. I miss her greatly. Not a day goes by that I don't think of her."

"Well I am nobody's mother," said Miss Temple pulling her shoulders back. "In answer to my question, have you caught anybody? Am I to continue to live in fear that someone is going to break in? Am I to lie awake at night listening for someone to use a screw driver on my front door lock? I noticed the last time you came you didn't take any fingerprints. What have you to say for yourself? What have you discovered? Don't patronize me."

"I wouldn't dream of it. What can I tell you?" said Clancy throwing up his hands. "There are some local youths that are breaking into homes. They are very hard to catch. By the time the police get there, they are long gone, vanished into the night. We have tried to track them down but so far we have not been successful. It takes time."

"Unlike yourself, I haven't got time. I could be murdered in my bed."

"Have you thought of installing an alarm system in your home? Quite a few homes have them. The alarm sounding would frighten burglars away."

"I can't afford that. I am a poor pensioner, barely getting by." She clutched her purse to her chest more closely.

"What about having someone live with you, move in, a friend or relative?"

Miss Temple responded sharply, "I prefer my own company, thank you. I always have and I always will."

"I see," said Clancy. He sighed. "We could have a patrol car go by your house every so often just to check on things. Would that help?"

"It would give me some feeling of security to know that the police were taking an interest. I am a tax payer like everyone else. I need peace of mind."

"Is there anything else on your mind?"

"No, that will do for the moment," said Miss Temple preparing to leave. "Good day."

Clancy went down the hall and rapped on the toilet door. "You can come out now, Greg. She's gone."

"Thank heavens," said Greg.

"She's still stewing about the attempted burglary. But the bump on the head has wiped out her memory of the men who stole her purse and hit her on the head on the Trans Canada Trail. All she can remember is her hospital stay. She can't describe these men, so catching them is a bit iffy."

David came back into the room after being out on an errand for a few minutes.

"What was that all about? Why was Hugh Jones so angry?" asked David "What is this scoop that Mira got? Am I missing something?"

"That was a power play, nothing more, nothing less made by Hugh Jones. Lawyers always like to throw their weight around. It's part of their DNA."

"I'm confused. There have been some changes that I am not aware of. Fill me in on what is going on. Do you have a few minutes?"

"Better get yourself a coffee. I am going to get one, too."

Clancy settled himself down in his chair. David still holding up his coffee brought another chair up to his. Outside it was raining, He could hear the pings of rain on the roof and the windows. What had happened to change Clancy's mind.

"What have you figured out about Holly Jones that got her husband so angry?" asked David. "Why have you arrested her and put her in jail pending other charges? Last time I spoke to you, you thought it was Brenda Lang who had done it. I am all ears."

"I made a mistake. I thought Brenda had done it. All

signs pointed to Brenda, so I thought. This time I am sure who did it. But making it murder one might prove difficult. There is not enough evidence. It's all circumstantial. We never found the murder weapon, the knife. For motive, we have Miss Sweet who will declare that Holly Jones had the hots for Dr. Lang. Our most important witness, Brenda Lang saw her down on the trail around the time that Dr. Lang was murdered. When she took an overdose, I finally realized that Brenda couldn't have done it. She loved her husband too much and would never have killed him. The only person that she hated was Miss Sweet her rival. That was the person she could have gladly killed because Miss Sweet was stealing her husband."

Clancy paused to take a sip of coffee.

"Go on," said David.

"Dr. Lang was a very attractive man. All his life, Dr. Lang had no shortage of women. He attracted them like flies, because he said nothing. He asked them a lot of questions and then listened politely when they answered no matter how boring the answers were. He let them do the talking. The women felt important that this psychiatrist, with all the degrees after his name, was listening to them.

He was like a mirror. The women projected their love and sexual fantasies onto him. They never really got to know him as a person because he said little about himself. But in his relationships with real women he couldn't sustain the relationship which require the skills of warmth and intimacy. Bored with his first wife, Evelyn he divorced her to marry Brenda, a nurse, whose insecurities about their relationship made her soon take to drink. Was he happy or unhappy, she didn't know because he never said anything. He confided his marital problems to Miss Sweet who offered tea and sympathy. In the far off future, he may have hoped eventually to leave Brenda and marry Miss Sweet. Brenda got wind of his flirtation and threatened Miss Sweet a couple of times."

Just then the phone rang. "Greg will you take it? I am busy explaining something to David. Now where were we? While this was going on, a patient, Mrs. Jones, had become enamored of Dr. Lang during her psychotherapy sessions. I hear that the government is cutting back on funding for this kind of therapy. There are so few psychiatrists available. Most of them at the hospitals are dealing now with seniors having dementia and teens overdosing on drugs."

"You are getting sidetracked," said David.

Clancy took another sip of coffee and cleared his throat. "Dr. Lang rebuffed her, both for professional reasons and also I believe for personal reasons. She wasn't his type. As a woman she was too hard and too aggressive. Her ego couldn't take no for an answer. She wanted more from Dr. Lang; going.to therapy once a week wasn't enough. She found out that he jogged on the Trans Canada Trail. So that Friday she went out jogging hoping to meet up with him on the Trans Canada Trail.

"Now Holly is a narcissistic individual who can't take rejection. She can't take no for an answer. Even as an adult, she is childlike in never having to accept or face responsibility for her actions. She's a bit of a sociopath. Her husband Hugh has resumed the role of parent, protecting her, smoothing her way out of jams, and calming the waters. She has never faced jail time for her shop lifting. She has never had to face reality. This is the way I figured it. It wasn't a deliberately planned murder as such. It was an impulse, an act of desperation."

"Holly Jones? Hugh Jones's wife. I never would have fingered her."

"Two people can place her there. Jimmy Snipe saw her car heading down to the lake and Brenda saw her on the trail. Unfortunately for Dr. Lang, she did meet up with him. This is the scenario as I picture it. She suggested that they jog together. But he demurred. Next she suggested that they meet to have a coffee afterwards. Again he put her off. She was pressing for more time with him, more time outside of the office. He probably told her flat out, that he just was not interested.

"Her ego couldn't take it. She couldn't take him saying no to her. So she took the knife out of the granny pack and stabbed him when he turned around. I don't think she meant to kill him, just threaten him. He fell to the ground. Not knowing whether he was dead or not, she dragged him into the bushes. She was a tall, strong woman and this would present no difficulty. If he was dead, she hoped that he would not be found for some time. She had to move quickly. She had just enough time, less than twenty minutes to do this and then get back to the house and establish an alibi to appear to have been there all afternoon.

"Will she get life? Twenty five years?"

"I doubt it. There is not enough solid evidence to convict her of murder one. There is just not enough evidence." said Clancy grimacing. "It is all circumstantial at best. It wasn't premeditated as such. I don't think she meant to kill him, just threaten him, just scare him. It was meant to show her power over him. Then things got out of hand. In any case, her husband will plead diminished responsibility, the fact she was seeing a psychiatrist and was high on drugs. I can see her doing ten if that, more like three years with time off for good behavior."

"We're too soft on the criminals. Every criminal is treated like a victim. It is disgusting."

"You can say that again. There is one law for the rich and one for the poor. Being a nut case is even better if you want to commit murder. Look at that guy down in Toronto who killed a police officer with a snow plow. He got sentenced to a psychiatric hospital in Whitby. Pending therapy sessions and the psychiatrists' evaluations, he's eligible now for day passes despite the protests of the widow and the police union. They're calling on the prime minister to do something about it."

"I hear that Brenda is out of intensive care," said David.

"She will manage alright. Dr. Coldwater is a widower and I can see them teaming up. Misery likes company. I hope Dr. Coldwater recommends a treatment program for her drinking. As for Miss Sweet, things will be more difficult for her for the first little while. She's out of a job and out of a future husband. Finding a new partner will have its challenges in a small town with few men available."

"Bring me up to scratch on Miss Temple, Clancy. What are you going to do about the thugs who broke into Miss Temple's cottage, hit her on the head and stole her purse and left her in a ditch, not that they are the same perpetrators? Has anything happened in that investigation?"

"You're asking me an embarrassing question. Picture this scenario and it's the only scenario we've got so far. We have no evidence to convict. We know that most break-ins are drug related, thieves' looking for easy cash and that is Jimmy Snipe's crowd. It's hard to catch them at it. Picture this as to what happened that day. It's the only plausible explanation that I can give you.

Our little old lady, Miss Temple decides to go for a little afternoon stroll along the Trans Canada Trail to look at the wildflowers, to admire the birds and the bees, and just wander along enjoying the nice weather. She is just out doing a little day-dreaming. Then all of a sudden she stops when she spots two young men in jeans with their hoodies hiding their faces, huddled together in the middle of the trail. They looked over their shoulders suspiciously as she approached them. She calls out, "Good afternoon, gentlemen, lovely weather we're having.'

One says, "Yeh, what's it to you, you old bugger."

"Such vile language." She exclaimed. "I was only asking, just asking. Is that what I think it is?" She pointed to the reefer in his mouth. "Are you selling drugs on this beautiful woodland trail?"

"Bugger off, old lady, if you know what is good for you."

"But like a hungry dog she wouldn't let go of the bone. She made a pest of herself, putting herself in harm's way, protesting to their being there and drug dealing. For her interference, she gets whacked on the head and dumped in the ditch at the side of the road and left unconscious. It is a coincidence that Dr. Lang came by later just missing all this action by maybe ten minutes. We will never know who whacked her on the head. Probably the same guys who shot Jimmy Snipes in the thigh in the park. I think they might be the same ones that broke into her cottage. And then took off. It's a shady world out there. We are operating in the shadows of society.

"Should we spend the energy tracking them down? We have no physical description of them. Miss Temple with her banged up head is not a good witness and she has temporary amnesia. The defense lawyer would chew her up. We have no evidence, no fingerprints on the purse because we didn't think to look for them and besides they would be covered with that young girl's prints and her mother's.

"I ask you should we bother with those fleas. Sooner or later they will fall into our hands if they keep breaking into homes. We will catch them if they don't kill each other first. Jimmy Snipe is lucky that he only got a gunshot wound to the thigh. Most drug users eventually get killed and this saves us a lot of trouble, a lot of court time and public money.

With no evidence, no reliable witnesses, we are at a standstill. That's what it's worth."

"I guess you are right. But it had one good outcome. If we hadn't gone looking for her, Dr. Lang's body would have been there for days."

"You're right on that one."

"It's time for a break. I need to stretch my legs. I might walk down the street to Apple Annie's."

"Thanks for the info. I'm up to speed now," said David.

Clancy got up from his chair, picked up his jacket and headed out. He whistled happily to himself thinking all's well that ends well.

It was 3 p.m. The place was buzzing with pantsuits, blazers and trousers, and ladies in pearls and frilly chiffon summer dresses, matrons in white shorts and flip flops and the odd old lady who had walked in from the country for exercise. He nodded to the customers as he went in. No one he recognized as he passed them by. Then towards the back he stopped. He recognized a familiar face and headed there.

"May I join you?"

Miss Sweet gave him an unhappy look. "Do you want to socialize with a murder suspect? Isn't that a conflict of interest or are you here to ask more questions?" Miss Sweet's cornflower blue eyes burned into his.

'No, Miss Sweet, this is a social call. I'm just being friendly. Would you like a second cup of coffee?"

Miss Sweet shook her head." I'm not in the mood for it."

"I am here to tell you something important," He slid

into the seat beside her.

"Yes, what is it?"

"We have arrested the murder suspect, someone you know."

"Someone I know?"

"Yes, a patient of Dr. Lang, Mrs. Holly Jones."

"I knew it was her. That bitch. I hope they hang her. Hell is not hot enough for her."

"Wishful thinking, Miss Sweet but the courts will do the best they can to mete out justice. I thought you should know."

"Dr. Lang did so much to help her and this is how she thanked him. She had no gratitude. Ruthless bitch."

"Yeh, well you did a lot to help Miss Sweet, it wouldn't have been possible for this investigation to proceed without you." He gave her a big smile. "I hope there is no misunderstanding lingering between the two of us?"

Miss Sweet blushed, "I will accept your offer of a second cup of coffee."

CPSIA information can be obtained at www.ICGtesting.com
Printed in the USA
LVOW08s1744210116

471717LV00007B/675/P